SAMMS
AGENDA

The
SAMMS
AGENDA

ALISON KENT

KENSINGTON PUBLISHING CORP.
http://www.kensingtonbooks.com

BRAVA BOOKS are published by

Kensington Publishing Corp.
850 Third Avenue
New York, NY 10022

All Kensington titles, imprints and distributed lines are available at special quantity discounts for bulk purchases for sales promotion, premiums, fund-raising, educational or institutional use.

Special book excerpts or customized printings can also be created to fit specific needs. For details, write or phone the office of the Kensington Special Sales Manager: Kensington Publishing Corp., 850 Third Avenue, New York, NY 10022. Attn. Special Sales Department. Phone: 1-800-221-2647.

Brava and the B logo Reg. U.S. Pat. & TM Off.

ISBN 0-7582-0672-0

First Kensington Trade Paperback Printing: December 2004
10 9 8 7 6 5 4 3 2 1

Printed in the United States of America

A man can stand a lot as long as he can stand himself. He can live without hope, without friends, without books, even without music, as long as he can listen to his own thoughts.

—Axel Munthe, 1857–1949
Swedish physician, psychiatrist, and writer

The
SAMMS
AGENDA

One

Turning heads was something Katrina Flurry had done constantly throughout the twenty-eight years of her life. She wasn't going to apologize for it, defend it, or get bent out of shape when it didn't sit well with what girlfriends she had left.

She'd never been one to play up her looks, but she'd certainly never had a reason to play them down. Especially now that they were one of the only things left she had going for her. Sad that such was the state of things, but running from the truth went against her personal grain.

Even if lately she'd given the idea of running a whole lot of thought.

Her looks had played a big part in her successful entrée into the social circles about which she wrote. In fact, her syndicated urban lifestyle column, *Cosmopolitan Arm Candy,* ran in a multitude of publications along with a caricature that looked enough like her to stop traffic dead.

And speaking of dead . . .

She swung her legs over the side of her lounger, slipped

her feet into her poolside slides, and packed her towel, sunscreen, and the paperback she'd been reading into her tote, wondering as she gathered up her things if her ex, the worthless bastard, had yet been sent to meet his maker.

It was true that Peter Deacon had provided amazing fodder for her column. And she wasn't about to deny how much she'd enjoyed spinning through the circles of society in which he'd traveled.

What she hadn't enjoyed was discovering two months ago that the man she'd dated for the six months prior wasn't who she'd thought he was at all.

That he was, in fact, the front man for the sort of crime syndicate that brought to mind James Bond movies and Elmore Leonard books—and which made her, ugh, his moll.

A mobster's girlfriend. What a lovely experience to add to her resumé.

She wondered with a rather grim satisfaction how Peter was enjoying his traveling now, from his cell to the prison mess hall and on to the caged exercise yard.

The thought of his well-manicured hands working to press license plates . . .

She leaned down to check the scuffed polish on one toe, feeling the zip of a bee zinging by her ear as she bent. Dodging the insect and cupping that side of her head, she swore never again to spend a free afternoon poolside after a morning pedicure.

Now she was going to need a touch-up before tonight's charity fund-raiser hosted by the Miami Symphony. She was so looking forward to an evening spent at the fabulous Mandarin Oriental without the odious and criminal Peter Deacon at her side.

Okay, she mused wryly, getting to her feet. She hadn't found him odious while they were seeing each other. At the time, however, she'd had no idea of his true colors—colors that now were now limited to black and white horizontal stripes, or whatever dazzling combination was worn by the population at Sing Sing.

Considering she would never be paying him a visit, she contented her imagination with picturing him thus—when she pictured him at all, an event growing more and more rare of late.

Adjusting the rise of her bikini bottoms, she reached for her cover-up and slipped it on, tightening the kimono's sash around her waist.

As much as she wished she could wipe him from her mind completely, a part of her harbored no small degree of guilt . . . or anger . . . or disgust—she had yet to define the emotion—that he'd pulled the wool over her eyes until she saw nothing but soft and cuddly sheep.

It was tough accepting that she'd been such a bad judge of character when she prided herself on the opposite.

She reached down for her tote, cringing again as that damn bee buzzed the hairs on the back of her neck. A big red welt of a sting would ruin the effect of the plunging ivory and gold silk halter topping the slim ankle-length Cleopatra skirt it had taken her hours to choose for tonight.

The fund-raising event was dreadfully important to her personal future as it was the first society function she would be attending unescorted since Peter's arrest.

The gossip would be flowing as freely as the Veuve Clicquot and Pol Roger, and squashing rumors of her knowledge of his true business dealings was her main goal for the evening.

She had not been a party, knowing, willing, or otherwise, to his unscrupulous activities, and she had certainly known nothing about his treasonable crimes.

Even now she shuddered and swallowed the bile that rose when she thought of the young scientist who'd burned to death in that fire in upstate New York. Rumor had the kid as deeply involved as Peter had been, but no one deserved such a horrific end.

At the môment, though, it was her own reputation on the line, her own future suffering the collateral damage of Peter's reach.

Courtney David, Katrina's editor at her home base of the *Miami Herald,* had warned her earlier in the week to expect a possible backlash. Two of the more conservative markets running *Cosmopolitan Arm Candy* had already put her column on hiatus until the hoopla of her involvement with Peter died down.

Repositioning her sunglasses, Katrina admitted she had a hell of a fight ahead. What her doubters and detractors didn't know was that fighting—and winning—was the hallmark of all Flurry women.

She would not lose the career she'd worked her ass off to establish without a serious battle royal and a lot of metaphorical dead bodies left in her wake.

It was when the bee buzzed her again and smashed into one of the poolside's Grecian urn planters that she realized the first dead body might very well be hers. Because that bee was no bee.

It was a bullet.

"Tzao gao," swore Julian Samms under his breath, the fluid burst of Mandarin as natural as picking the lock on the front door of Katrina Flurry's condo.

He wasn't worried about being caught on tape by the high-tech security system. Even a zoom shot would show him opening the door with what looked like a key.

Besides, though she didn't yet know it, Katrina Flurry didn't live here anymore.

And if he didn't get her out of Miami now, she wouldn't be living at all.

Spectra IT, the international crime syndicate tailor-made to employ scum like Peter Deacon, had put out a hit on the man's former girlfriend, using the assassin most suited to a job involving a sexy woman and a gun: Benny Rivers.

Julian knew way too much about Benny's penchant for abhorrent sexual torture. The other man was an equal opportunity sadist, meaning no man, woman, or sheep was safe from the abuse and humiliation he doled out before death.

Hank Smithson, the founder and principal of the Smithson Group, had sent Julian to make sure Katrina avoided that scenario while Mick Savin, Hank's newest SG-5 recruit, put his bloodhound nose to Benny's foul trail.

If the game went according to plan, and she didn't put up an uncooperative stink in the process, Julian would have Katrina tucked safely away thirty minutes from now.

He knew from his surveillance that she was home; he'd hoped a simple knock would've been enough to gain him entrance. But no. Either she wasn't opening up because she hadn't recognized him, or because she was busy in her closet alphabetizing her shoes by designer.

He had absolutely no problem with quality footwear; he had a problem with any obsession resulting in waste of any kind—physical, mental, emotional, or spiritual.

The fact that she could afford a real-life *Sex and the City* wardrobe had no impact on his opinion. But then, nothing ever did. Nothing ever would.

Not after what he'd witnessed during the two years he'd spent stationed in Africa.

And on that last deadly assignment in Kenya.

He'd read several installments of her syndicated column during his mission prep. *Cosmopolitan Arm Candy.* What a load of high-maintenance *gou shi*. The fact that she had the readership she did left him speechlessly shaking his head at the state of female affairs.

If women thought men gave a rat's ass about external trappings, they were out of their airheaded minds.

Men who were real men cared about two things. A woman able to carry on an intelligent conversation filled with innuendo and mind games, who then delivered an equally fulfilling challenge once she joined him in bed.

The makeup and jewelry and shoes and nails? Uh-uh. His experience told him those were tools used to impress other women and for gaining an edge in the self-esteem war games females played.

Why they felt the strangely competitive need to best one another with the superficial trappings of class . . . He gave another shake of his head as the door came open in his hand.

He didn't want to walk in and find himself facing the wrong end of the handgun registered in her name, so he knocked again as he cracked open the door. "Miss Flurry?"

He peered into the foyer. *Whoa. Nice digs,* he mused, stepping onto white-and-black marbled Italian tile. He knew from his background research that Katrina came from money, that her father had died while she was in high school, leaving wife and daughter financially set for the rest of their lives.

His bitching about her wardrobe budget aside, he had to admire her taste. Talk about quality. He'd even give her elegance. Her place deserved a spread in *Architectural Digest.* He figured her square footage at two thousand at least— not a bad bit of acreage for one person to move around in.

She went for what he supposed was classical, or traditional, the sort of décor that didn't exactly invite anyone to sit, to ditch their shoes, to kick back with a beer and spend Sunday afternoon watching football—a nonissue since the room didn't have a television and he wouldn't fit on her red and gold brocade camelback sofa anyway.

You're a moron, Samms. You're not a fixture in her condo or in her life. And it would never be so with any woman, a fact his subconscious was still warring over with his logic all these years later.

A cursory walk-through of her kitchen yielded no Katrina, no dirty dishes, and nothing on the stove. A perverse part of him wanted to check her refrigerator, see if it was stocked with fruits, vegetables, yogurt, and designer-label water, but the unsealed package of Chunky Chips Ahoy on the countertop changed his mind. Not to mention intrigued him.

He liked the idea of this gourmet woman having a few pedestrian tastes. It made him wonder how she'd feel about eating those cookies in bed—yet another mental detour he had no business taking.

He made his way over the plush ivory carpet toward the private rooms of the condo. "Miss Flurry?"

Still nothing, and yeah, he'd been right on the mark with his earlier assessment of the money she spent on shoes. Standing at the door to her monstrous closet, he estimated she owned a hundred pair.

A regular mini-Imelda.

And he really shouldn't be checking out her wardrobe, but it was either that or the bed. The bed which made him think about those cookies and how he could really go for a night of down and dirty sex.

He headed back to the living room and the balcony that opened over the courtyard pool. The fitness center and tennis courts would be his next destination since he knew she employed a housekeeper and wouldn't be doing her own laundry in the center's facilities . . .

There she was, down at the pool, her back to him as she got to her feet and tugged at a pair of bikini bottoms that sent his libido back to the idea of leaving cookie crumbs in her bed.

She'd coiled her shoulder-length caramel-colored hair

into a knot on top of her head. He liked the length of her neck almost as much as he liked the length of her legs.

What he wasn't crazy over was the way she was covering up without first turning around so he could get a full frontal view of that body. Then again, her body was merely a perk of this job, not the reason he was here.

She looked like she was on her way back upstairs, meaning he'd do better to intercept her on the other side of her front door. Save himself a buttload of explaining—who he was, how he'd gotten in, what he wanted, as well as the hassle of having to restrain her when she refused to listen.

Cookies or not, she struck him as the type to act first and ask questions a mile or so down the damn road.

In the next second, however, the insect she'd been dodging shot his carefully laid plans to shit when the cement planter it hit exploded. Julian whipped his gaze to the rooftop across from where he stood.

Sunlight cast Benny Rivers's block-like head in silhouette, and glinted off the barrel of the rifle aimed her way.

Katrina's only saving grace for the moment was that Rivers never gave his prey an easy time, toying with his victims, making them sweat out the wait for their death.

Heart pounding in the base of his throat, Julian gauged the distance from the balcony to the manicured lawn edging the poolside walk, gauged the distance to the deep end of the crystal blue water shimmering in the sun, chose the lesser of two evils, and jumped.

Two

Julian hit the ground with a jolt, seams ripping, bones crunching, joints popping as he rolled to his feet and came up into a full-throttle run.

Coattails flying, he sprinted across the pool's cement deck, hurdled the shattered planter, and gave Katrina no chance to do more than gasp her surprise as he grabbed her upper arm and ran.

"Go! Go! Go! Go! Go!"

He propelled her forward, knowing he could run a hell of a lot faster then she could, the both of them dragged down even more by the *slap, slap, slap* of her ridiculous shoes.

She seemed to reach the very same conclusion at the very same time, however, and kicked off the slides to run in bare feet.

Once across the deck and up the courtyard stairs, he shoved open the enclosure's gate. Another bullet ricocheted off the iron railing.

Katrina screamed, but kept up with the pace he set as

they pushed through and barreled down the arched walk-way toward the parking garage.

Her Lexus was closer, but he doubted she had her keys and didn't have time to stop, ask, and wait for her to dig them from the bottom of her bag.

Even breaking in, hot-wiring would take longer than the additional burst of speed and extra twenty-five yards they'd need to reach his Benz.

"My car. Let's go," he ordered.

She followed, yelping once, cursing once, twice, yet sticking by his side all the way.

A shot cracked the pavement to the right of their path, a clean shot straight between two of the garage's support beams. Way too close for comfort.

Rivers's practice was about to make perfect in ways Julian didn't want to consider.

The keyless transponder in his pocket activated the entry into his car from three feet away. He touched the handle, jerked open the SL500's driver's side door.

Katrina scrambled across the console, tossed her bag onto the floor; he slid down into his seat, punched the ignition button, shoved the transmission into reverse.

Tires screaming, he whipped backwards out of the parking space and shot down the long row of cars. He hit the street ass-backwards, braked, spun, shifted into first, and floored it, high-octane adrenaline fueling his flight.

Halfway down Grand, several near misses and an equal number of traffic violations later, he cast a quick sideways glance at Katrina and nodded. "You might want to buckle up."

She cackled like she'd never heard anything more ridiculous. "You're suggesting that now?"

He shrugged, keeping an eye on his rearview and any unwanted company, whether Rivers or the cops. He wasn't about to stop for either. "Better late than never."

That earned him a snort, but she did as she'd been told. Then she lifted her left foot into her lap, giving him an eye-ful of a whole lotta tanned and toned thigh. "I've got glass in my foot."

He didn't say anything. He had to get out of her neigh-borhood and ditch his car—a reality that seriously grated. "Stitches?"

She shook her head, leaning down for a closer look at the damage. "I don't think so. Tweezers, antibiotic ointment, and a bandage should suffice."

"I've got a first aid kit in the trunk." How many times had he patched himself up on the fly? "I'll grab it as soon as we stop. In the meantime . . ." He pulled his handkerchief from his pocket.

"Thanks." She halved it into a triangle and wrapped her foot securely, knotting the fabric on top at the base of her toes. "When you hit 95, head south. The police station's on Sunset."

He nodded, turned north at the next intersection.

"Uh, hello? I said Sunset. South, not north."

"I heard you." This wasn't the time for a long explana-tion as to why he couldn't go to the police, why SG-5 couldn't risk exposure.

Why he'd learned a long time ago that actions spoke a hell of a lot louder than words.

"Look," she said, settling her sunglasses that he hap-pened to know were Kate Spade firmly in place. "I appreci-ate the save, even if I was dumb as a stick to get in this car not knowing who you are. But we're going to the police, or I'll be making a scene like you wouldn't believe."

Oh, he believed Miss High Maintenance capable of some-thing that *feng le* . . . crazy. So far the only surprise had been her lack of complaints over their full out hundred-yard dash and the injury she'd sustained in the process.

"This isn't a police matter." Still, heading in the direction of the station might keep Rivers at bay and give Julian time to consider his options.

"And why would that be?" she asked, her incredulous tone of voice unable to mask the sound of the gears whirring in her mind. "You're with the shooter, aren't you? This kidnapping was the goal all along. You sonofabitch."

Julian couldn't help it. He smiled. It was something he rarely did for good reason, and the twitch of unused facial muscles felt strange.

But there was just something about a woman with a sailor's mouth that grabbed hold of his gut and twisted him up with the possibilities.

He hadn't had a really good mouth in a very long time.

A thought that sobered him right up. "No. I'm not with the shooter. His name is Benny Rivers. He's with Spectra IT and he's in Miami to take you out."

Take her out. As in . . . kill her?
Dead?

"Who are you?" she asked, her pulse fluttering like it hadn't since she'd first learned the truth of Peter Deacon's affiliations.

Fluttering harder, in fact, if fluttering was even the right word considering if felt like a jackhammer pounding away in her chest. "What do you want?"

"What I want is to keep you alive." He shifted down, revved his RPMs. The car shot up the ramp onto I-95. "Who I am isn't as important."

"Uh, if my life is in danger then what's important is my call to make." Her foot begin to throb, the glass shard suddenly taking on the dimensions of a Fifth Avenue window in Bergdorf's.

"My name is Julian Samms," he finally answered in that voice that sounded like honey poured over a shattered mirror. Smooth and ragged all at the same time.

"Julian Samms. And you're simply an ordinary average concerned citizen?" He was obviously nothing of the sort.

Was, in fact, much much more, what with his very sophisticated James Bond attire, not to mention his car, which was worth a small fortune, and his skill behind the wheel.

Ordinary average concerned citizens did not drive like highly trained bats out of hell.

"Something like that," he responded, whipping through traffic with one eye trained on his mirrors, one hand on the wheel, and the other on the gear shift as he searched the road behind.

She wanted to glance back, to see what he was looking for, but what really mattered was what lay ahead. "Where are we going?"

"I'm not sure."

"What do you mean, you're not sure?" How could he have been in the right place at the right time and not be sure of what he was doing now?

"Exactly what I said." Another in-and-out maneuver that had her grabbing hold of the door. "All I know is that I've got to get you out of Miami."

"For how long?"

"As long as it takes."

"As long as what takes?"

The glance he cast her way accused her of asking too many stupid questions for a woman on the run for her life.

Logically, she knew that. Emotionally . . .

"I can't leave. I work here. I live here," she said, hysteria adding an ugly shrillness to her voice. And tonight was the fund-raiser!

He ignored her panic and simply said, "You used to live here."

No. She was not going to listen to this or go down without a fight.

She was already struggling to regain the personal and career footing she'd lost by having her name linked with an international crime figure.

And at that thought . . .

Dear God, but she was in serious trouble here, wasn't she? More trouble than she'd been willing to accept until it was slapped brutally across her face like a bullwhip.

Or like a bullet.

She slumped back, deflated, defeated, yet determined to find a better solution than one calling for her to give up everything she still held dear.

"I don't understand why we can't go to the police." She didn't understand anything at all! "Surely they could provide me protection."

Julian snorted. "The same way they provided you protection from Rivers?"

"How could they when they didn't know . . . ?"

But he had known. Julian Samms had known. Which brought her back to the moment's biggest conundrum.

Who the hell was this dangerous man and what about him made her feel safe when the circumstances should have her feeling anything but?

She shifted in her seat as best she could to face him, studying his profile as he concentrated on the traffic and the road.

The shoulder seam of his black Hugo Boss suit was torn, the fabric separating now as his muscles bunched while he shifted gears, revealing the white shirt he wore, also torn and showing a hint of deeply tanned skin underneath.

She couldn't tell much about his body beyond the fact that he ran a hell of a lot faster than she would've imagined for a man of his size. He was very large. Intimidatingly so.

Or would have been had she been put off by physical strength.

She never had been, she mused, the faint hum of the wheels on the pavement belying the speed at which they traveled. Since childhood, she'd used her wits to get out of any scrapes she'd been in, believing brains won out over brawn every time.

She believed it still to this day. And she needed to employ the same wits now she had then, but wasn't having as easy a time of it.

As far as she knew, no one had ever tried to kill her before.

"Do you have any sort of plan then?" she finally asked, because staring at the thick dark hair pulled into a tail at his nape was getting her nowhere.

His answer was a sharp vocal burst in a language she did not understand and an equally sharp spin of the steering wheel. The movement took them across all the lanes of traffic, down the exit ramp, and into the parking lot surrounding the Shops at Sunset Place.

He slipped the car into a spot between two oversized SUVs, set the emergency brake, and left the car idling in neutral. "We've got to switch cars."

She could help with that, she realized. She could finally help with something. "I can get us a car."

His head swiveled her way. His blue eyes burned beneath brows even blacker than his hair. But it was the tight line of his lips, the stress brackets on either side of his mouth that drew her gaze.

"What sort of car and where?"

She shook her head. She obviously wasn't going to draw this out, but there were things she needed to know.

And she needed to know them now. "I'll tell you. As soon as you answer a few questions for me."

Three

Julian never talked about who he was, where he'd come from, what he did. "What sort of questions?"

"I would think that would be obvious," she said, the defensive arch of her brow a tactical maneuver made to unbalance him.

It failed, of course, ramping up his curiosity about her instead.

He wondered if she thought the look was enough to mask the swell of fear she was riding. He knew fear, recognized it, would've smelled it on her if not for all the other scents swirling in the car's interior.

Sunscreen and sweet soap and the soft citrus tang of her hair.

When it became clear that he wasn't going to answer what he hadn't been asked, both her expression and her tone of voice shifted from imperious to insistent.

"Who are you that you know more about Spectra IT's activities than the police do?"

"The group I work for . . ." He hesitated, not wanting to

say enough to give away SG-5 but knowing she deserved this much of the truth—needed it, in fact, if they were both to stay alive. "One of my associates is responsible for taking your ex out of commission."

She blinked once, twice, her lashes long, sable dusted with gold. "Are you government? Military?"

He shook his head. "Not any longer."

"I don't get it," she said, her eyes reflecting the anger and confusion warring behind. "I mean, I understand what you're doing here, but I don't get who sent you or why or who you work for—"

"You don't need to get it. All you need to do is stay alive until Rivers is disposed of." That and follow his orders without the back talk and sass he'd geared up for. Neither of which he'd yet seen.

She met his gaze squarely, her chin quivering so slightly he doubted she noticed. "And that's where you come in, right? The keeping me alive part."

He nodded. It was Mick Savin who would be disposing of Benny Rivers, though Julian still wasn't clear why Hank had given the new recruit the meatier task while assigning him to baby-sit.

He draped his left wrist over the steering wheel and tried not to notice the way the diamond studs in her ears glittered, or the way her topknot sat askew, strands of hair curling wildly the length of her neck.

Caramel strands. Caramel and chocolate. Chocolate chip cookies. He stifled a groan. "Anything else?"

She canted her head, looked down and picked at the handkerchief bandage. "We only dated casually. Peter and I. We were never a romantic item."

"Right." Julian turned his head, moved his gaze to the rearview mirror, searching for any possible sign of Rivers instead of divining the truth from her eyes.

That particular truth, her relationship with Deacon, didn't matter.

"I never slept with him."

Her soft confession had Julian grinding his jaw. "Sure. Whatever."

She sighed with a heavy sense of even heavier frustration. "I hate people thinking that more went on between us than actually did."

It didn't matter, he told himself again. *It didn't matter.* Her association with and her obvious attraction to the Spectra sleazebag was enough to turn Julian right off, chocolate chip cookies aside.

He drummed his fingertips on the dash. "What about the car?"

"My mother lives in Coral Gables. She's in London visiting friends. I have keys to her place and to her car."

"You have them with you?"

She muttered a faint string of foul words under her breath. "No. They're at my condo."

"Rivers will be watching the place anyway."

"How would he know—" She cut herself off before saying more, took a deep breath. "Never mind. I'm just glad she's not there."

If she had been, Julian would've taken measures to keep her out of harm's way. "Don't worry about it. The car part, I mean."

Again she pulled at the knot on the bandage. "I thought you covert types always had contingency plans."

His plan had been to set her up in a safe house until Rivers was no longer an issue. A safe house hidden on the tip of the peninsula that put SG-5 within spitting distance of Spectra's offshore activities.

The plan remained the same. It was Rivers who was going to make the execution tougher than Julian had hoped.

He pulled his cell phone from his waistband and hit his speed dial.

"Savin."

"It's Julian. Rivers is here. I just lost him on 95 out of Coconut Grove."

"Great." Mick bit off a sharp laugh. "Because I lost him up at Okeechobee."

"You'll be here soon?"

"Less than an hour."

"Good. *Zhu yi.*"

"Yeah. You watch your back, too."

Julian slapped the phone closed. "Sit tight. I'm going to get the first aid kit."

She nodded, her eyes as dry as the Chalbi Desert he knew too well. He pushed from the car, opened the trunk, thinking of the dry barren waste and the sun cooking a man's skin to a fiery red crisp.

Not toasting it to a golden brown tan that went on forever, inside her thighs and out, all the way to the scrap of parakeet yellow fabric between her legs that he knew would be sheer when wet.

It was the thinking of making her wet that had driven him from the car even more than the glass in her foot.

She wasn't his type—he'd met few women who were—but he was a man, and she was wearing next to nothing and smelling like sunshine and—*zing!*

Hun dan!

Sonofabitch! The bullet pierced the wheel well, whacked into the passenger door of the neighboring SUV.

Julian slammed the trunk, curses rolling from his tongue as he dashed forward. He threw the first aid kit into Katrina's lap, shifted into reverse, and whipped back out of the parking space.

He shot blindly down the row of parked cars, skidding into a ninety-degree turn at the end of the row. They'd be nothing but a moving target on 95, but getting to the safe house was paramount.

Pulse pounding, he tore out of the lot on what felt like two wheels, hit the lane to the interstate's entrance ramp prepared to top out the roadster at its 360 kilometers per hour.

Katrina dug fingertips into his thigh and stopped him with a manic, "U-turn! U-turn! Go back!"

He did what she said. She couldn't believe he'd done what she said—even as she swore she'd saved both their lives. God, but she could barely think to breathe.

She'd seen the hell-bent-for-leather expression darkening his face and feared he'd flip this rocket of a car, killing them both.

With that scenario now on hold, she directed him off the S. Dixie at 8th Avenue exit and had him turn east.

"Little Havana?"

"My mother and I employ the same housekeeper. We can use her car." She hesitated. "And leave her yours."

The glance he cast her remained indecipherable even after he'd returned his gaze to the road.

But the intensity stuck with her, and she couldn't help but wonder what he was thinking, considering he knew only the more salacious parts of her past.

"Besides, I've got to get clothes." On this she would not budge.

Nothing about the way he'd looked at her had been the least bit improper. But she could hear him breathe and sensed a tight discomfort, as if the distance between them was too little.

Or maybe too much.

She directed him through the neighborhood; his car, as she'd known it would do, turned heads, drawing more attention than she could tell he liked. The quick twists and turns they took through the narrow streets, however, would make their vanishing act hard to follow.

"Turn in here." She indicated Maribel's driveway. The housekeeper's sedan was parked at the curb. The one-car garage was empty. "Pull into the garage."

She answered the question asked by his dark expression. "Maribel's husband Tomas parks his truck in here. But I promise he won't mind if we store your car for now."

He eased the Mercedes roadster into the tiny pocket of space between tarps, ladders, plastic sheeting, and cans of paint.

He cut off the engine with the touch of a button, leaving her listening to the sound of her own heartbeat and what she swore was the equally rapid thrumming of his.

She wanted to turn to him, to demand more details than the scant ones he'd provided, to lean into the curve of his shoulder and rest her head. To pull the leather band from his nape and watch his thick black hair fall to frame his high cheekbones and strong jaw and . . .

Oh-kay. Enough with the fantasy. Time to get out of the car and start getting her life back, though she supposed tonight's fund-raiser was now out of the question. Damn but she'd looked good in that Cleopatra dress.

And damn that her nonappearance tonight would set additional tongues to wagging, creating more controversy she'd have to deal with eventually.

Feeling sorry for herself, however, was hardly productive when bigger things than her dress and reputation were being threatened. She wasn't exactly thrilled to add experience with gunfire and high-speed chases to her resumé.

Not to mention dealing with this ridiculous attraction to a man she wasn't yet sure was captor or savior.

The pit of her stomach tingling, she hobbled from the car to the backyard's chain-link gate. Holding the first aid kit in one hand, her tote in the other, she worked up the gate's horseshoe closure.

Behind her, Julian pulled down the garage's one-piece door. By the time she'd reached Maribel's back porch and knocked, he'd joined her. When nobody answered, she knocked again.

"She's usually home on Fridays. Should we wait?"

"No." He reached into his suit coat's inside pocket, withdrew a thin leather pouch stocked with what looked like dentistry tools but she knew were lock picks. "We're going in."

four

Little Havana, Friday, 4:30 P.M.

Katrina followed him though the door with no small amount of trepidation. Maribel would not mind in the least having them inside her house.

But the idea of breaking and entering like a common criminal did not sit well.

The white clapboard home's back entrance led directly into a small kitchen that was spotless. Knowing Maribel, Katrina expected no less.

She'd only been here once before, having brought food to the Gonzalez family when the housekeeper was called away by a relative's sudden death.

The gold-flecked linoleum was worn but waxed; the icebox and range both white enamel and from another era, functioning long past their prime.

The sink was white enamel, as well, chipped in spots but without a single stain. Katrina could see it all from where she still stood just inside the doorway.

Apparently much less ill at ease making his uninvited self at home, Julian vanished into the depths of the small house.

Katrina limped her way to the kitchen's Formica dinette set, pulled out a chair, and sat.

Placing her tote and the first aid kid on the tabletop, she lifted her foot to her lap and slipped off the knotted and bloody handkerchief.

Her foot was throbbing to beat the band. A quick inspection showed the sliver of glass to be a lot bigger and more deeply embedded than she'd thought.

Not that any thought beyond staying alive had been involved when she'd first felt the glass pierce her skin.

Sighing, she unzipped the canvas kit and had just found the tweezers when Julian tossed his torn shirt and coat across the table.

She glanced from the garments in need of repair to his face—but didn't make it that far. The heavy white T-shirt he'd pulled on to wear with his suit pants was all she could see.

No. That wasn't quite true. What filled her vision was the amazing expanse of his chest and the width of his shoulders poured into a shirt far too small.

He sat in the chair at a right angle to hers. Politeness forced her gaze to his face.

It was the clearest look she'd had of him so far, and she swore without hesitation that she'd never have climbed into his car if she'd seen him like this.

He'd pulled the band from his hair and the strands now hung to his shoulders; the color wasn't the pure black she'd thought, but a shade of brown just this side.

He patted his thigh. "Let me see your foot."

She lifted her heel to his knee, all too aware that she was wearing next to nothing and tucking the edges of the kimono as best she could over her thighs. "It's worse than I thought. I still don't think it needs stitches, but I'm not looking forward to digging for the glass."

Julian wrapped his fingers around her toes, bent them

back gently and tilted her foot. He studied the injury for a moment then turned to search the kitchen counters.

Katrina watched his face, ignoring the pressure and warmth of his fingers that had slipped down to ring her ankle. At least she told herself she was ignoring his touch.

Not that she believed anything she said considering the gooseflesh pebbling the entire length of her leg.

"Hang on a sec." He lifted her foot to the tabletop and pushed to stand, heading for the paper towels hanging from a roller next to the stove and the bottle of Cuervo Gold on top of the fridge. He didn't bother with glasses or ice.

It was when he sat down again that she realized the tequila was for her foot.

He braced the roll of paper towels on his thigh, reached for her heel, and propped it on top, scooting closer until her toes, if she flexed them, could tickle his ribs.

Flexing wasn't in the cards. Not when any movement now spit fire over the ball of her foot. She sucked in a sharp breath as Julian opened the bottle.

"This is gonna burn like a mother."

She gripped the aluminum edging along the seat of her chair and grit her teeth. "Bring it on."

He held her foot in one hand, held the bottle suspended in his other, and hesitated a moment while he also held her gaze.

His lips twitched with what might've been a spot of admiration. Unless it was devilish mischief. "Don't say I didn't warn you."

She stared into his eyes, the blue of a midnight sky. Blue and twinkling like those of a kid holding a match in one hand, a Black Cat in the other, and wondering if he could outrun the blast.

Interesting considering her insides seemed to be burning a similar fuse. A life-affirming sizzle detonating in the face of death. Oh, but this day was so not going well.

She inhaled deeply. "Hit me, bartender."

He poured. The alcohol ran from the ball of her foot down her sole and over her ankle to soak into the thick roll of towels. She wanted to scream but she couldn't. Not with Julian still holding her gaze.

Instead, she lifted one brow, gripped the chair even tighter, and nodded her permission for him to dig in. He took up the tweezers . . . and she never felt a thing.

He was good. Damn good. "I'm guessing you've had medic experience? More than simple Red Cross first aid?"

"I've seen a few guys get patched up, yeah. By medics, and by the Red Cross. None of it simple."

His attention on her foot, he wouldn't have noticed her silent touché. She offered it nonetheless. "How long were you in the service?"

He gave a strange shrug of his shoulders. "Six years. Almost."

She hissed sharply as the tweezers' tips grated over the edge of the glass. "That would be it."

"So it seems." He frowned, his dark brows drawing her attention to his eyes, to his nose, down to his lips.

He'd pressed them together as he concentrated; all she could think about was how much she wanted to kiss them. "Why almost?"

"Hmm?" He pulled the glass free, pressed his thumb to the gash to staunch the bleeding. "Why almost what?"

The pressure he applied created only marginally less pain than the glass. But it was a pain offset by the ridiculous pleasure his hands offered.

Good grief. What was the matter with her? "Why almost six years in the service?"

"You're going to need to be stitched up, but this will have to do for now." He replaced his thumb with a gauze pad. "Hold this a sec."

She leaned forward, held the gauze, watched while he uncapped the antibiotic ointment. His movements were precise and efficient as was his side of the conversation, an economy of words used to tell her nothing.

All he had to do was tell her to shut the hell up and quit asking questions, the answers to which were none of her business.

Then again, she mused, wincing only once as he applied the dressing, she was obviously projecting what she would be thinking were their positions reversed.

So it came as no small surprise when, while packing the items back into the kit, he said, "I was discharged. Dishonorably."

"What was the offense?" she heard herself asking.

Or maybe she wasn't hearing it at all but was only imagining what she would've asked had she found her voice.

Except that made no sense in light of his one-word answer.

"Murder."

Ten minutes later found Julian in the garage wondering if she'd believed him. If she thought he was trying to frighten her. If it had worked.

Or if she'd blown him off as a fuck-up. He wouldn't blame her if she had, considering he'd done such a piss poor job of losing Benny.

At least she'd found them a car that wasn't going to stand out on the road like a sore thumb.

Or a sore foot, he mused with no small bit of ironic humor while rummaging through the tools in the garage for anything he might need on the road.

He didn't care what Katrina said. She needed stitches. For now, the butterfly bandages he'd used would have to do.

His sewing skills were meant to save lives, not to pretty up an injury. He got within a meter of her with a needle, she'd need a televised extreme makeover.

He wondered if she'd bother repairing that sort of damage to the bottom of her foot. What he'd learned of her when prepping for this mission told him she'd have scheduled the surgery while on the run for her life.

What he'd learned of her since told him his intel was way off the mark.

High maintenance? Maybe. Spoiled princess? Not that he'd seen so far.

Sure their circumstances were way outside the realm of her norm. But they were also circumstances in which he'd have expected her to show her true colors—and he wasn't talking about that damned irritating parakeet yellow.

Leaving through the garage's side door, he headed back to the house, hoping Katrina had found something to wear and was ready to go, because they needed to move. This delay couldn't be helped, but it had taken time away from putting distance between themselves and Benny.

The quicker they reached the safe house, the fewer complications left in the way of Mick Savin taking out the Spectra IT shooter. The less complications distracting Julian from his agenda, as well.

The biggest distraction of all, the length of Katrina's naked legs in that damn bikini, had hopefully been taken care of by now.

She'd sworn she'd find something to wear, even if she had to dig through Tomas's wardrobe as well as Maribel's, what with Katrina being a nice five-foot-ten and Maribel reportedly eight inches shorter.

One step through the door and into the kitchen, however, had Julian barreling to a stop. Katrina's back was to him as she leaned over the countertop bar separating the kitchen from the small nook with the table and chairs.

She wore a pair of chunky athletic shoes, the left one unlaced and left loose over the thick sock and gauze wrapping binding her foot. Instead of the kimono, she wore a man's white dress shirt, sleeves cuffed to her elbows, hem knotted at her waist.

That left the rest of her, from ass to ankles, in a pair of indigo jeans way too big and obviously belonging to Tomas. She'd rolled the hems above the tops of the shoes and switched her hair from a topknot to a ponytail.

The look shouldn't have made him hard but it came goddamn close.

The way she'd shifted her weight to her right hip, the way the waistband of the Levi's rode low, the way a strip of smooth skin showed between the jeans and the shirttails had him thinking of handcuffs, silk ties, and old-fashioned hemp rope.

And chocolate chip cookies, as well.

He cleared his throat, held the tool tote he'd scavenged so that it covered his fly, and inclined his head when she glanced over her shoulder. "What're you doing?"

"Leaving Maribel a note and a check for the clothes"— her gaze dropped to the tool tote—"and I guess for whatever else you've borrowed."

"You have your checkbook with you?" A ridiculous thought but the only one that came to mind.

She nodded. "I always tuck my wallet in with my sunscreen and stuff. So I'll have my ID. I keep a spare key, too. That way I don't have to carry the whole ring to the pool."

"Hmph." He crossed to where she stood, set his tools next to her pool bag and a pair of fuzzy pink slippers she'd obviously filched, pulled his money clip from his pocket, and tossed three Benjamins on the counter. "I'll cover it."

"You don't have to do that."

"It's a business write-off. Don't worry about it." He pocketed the rest of his cash. "You have everything? We need to get gone."

"Let me finish this note—"

He pulled the paper from beneath her hand and read.

Maribel,

    I had an emergency and borrowed a few things. The money will cover the incidentals, and there's a car in the garage you should consider collateral until I return yours.

Katrina

Satisfied, he handed it back. "She'll know your handwriting?"

"She's worked for me for two years," she said, tearing the check she'd written from her checkbook. "She definitely knows my checks."

She'd matched his cash outlay to the penny. "I told you I'd cover it."

"I know you did." She dropped her wallet down into her tote and met his gaze. "But it was my bad choice in men responsible for this mess. Allow me to assuage at least a small measure of my guilt."

Buying her way out of her own bad judgment. Seems he hadn't been far off his original mark after all, he mused, offering a shrug that didn't convince him things were that cut and dried.

Especially since he found himself curling his fingers over his palm where the remembered feel of her slender foot nearly choked him. "Your prerogative."

"No, Julian." The smile on her lush lips grew twisted. "My multitude of sins."

five

Florida Turnpike, Florida City, Friday, 6:15 P.M.

A multitude of sins.

What a thing to confess to a murderer—if that's what he indeed was. What, not whom, because she refused to believe she was on the run with a man who held no regard for human life.

If that was the case, why go to the trouble to save hers when he didn't know her from Eve?

No. Julian Samms may have been responsible for people dying, but she would stake what reputation she had left that such incidents were line-of-duty, either military or with the covert organization for which he now worked.

She wanted to know more about him, about this unnamed group that kept tabs on men like Peter Deacon and the nefarious underworld through which his type circulated. Where they wheeled and dealed. Where they killed.

Dear God, she thought, and shivered, rubbing her palms up and down her arms to ward off the chill that had nothing to do with the temperature and everything to do with how unknowingly stupid she'd been.

"Cold?" Julian asked, reaching for the air conditioner controls on the sedan's dashboard panel.

She shook her head, glanced over. "I'm fine. As fine as possible considering this mess I've managed to create."

Julian didn't respond right away and she used the time to study his profile. His eyes, which were hidden behind sleek designer eyewear, dark narrow lenses in high-tech pewter frames. His lips, full yet unsmiling. His patrician nose, which she easily imagined on the silhouette of a statue in Rome.

He had cheekbones to die for, an uncompromising jaw, a warrior's long dark hair.

A warrior. Yes. That was it. That was exactly the man he brought to mind. Fierce and protective and dangerous, yet one she didn't fear. One with whom she felt safe.

One unlike any man she'd ever known—a thought that renewed the prickling sensation of gooseflesh, that roused tingles of awareness, a buzz of inappropriate sexual heat.

"You think you created it?"

"Excuse me?" She'd totally lost the drift of the conversation while indulging in her little chieftain/maiden fantasy.

"You said you created this mess."

"Well, yes." She shifted, cocked up her knee onto the seat and slipped the high-top from her swollen and bandaged left foot with a sharp hiss of breath. "Of all the men in all the cities in all the world, Peter Deacon had to be the one to walk into my life."

Julian snorted, then sobered. "Is that hurting much?"

"Which? My foot or my pride?"

"Your foot."

She nodded. "Throbbing a bit, but I'll live."

She caught the press of his lips as he battled speaking further, caught the surrender in the slack parentheses bracketing his mouth.

She couldn't help but smile when he gave in and asked, "And your pride?"

She shrugged. "What can I say? I've been better."

"Tough break," he said, switching lanes.

She turned her attention to the road and beyond. To the sawgrass prairie stretching into the deceptive nothingness of the Everglades. And because her pride was still an issue, she glanced back and changed the subject.

"Do you like what you do?"

"What I do?"

"Your job. Your career. Your calling."

He huffed, shifted to lean away from her, draped his right wrist over the steering wheel. Interesting, she mused, knowing whatever answer he might verbally offer would never be as telling as the language his body spoke.

Withdrawal. Self-preservation. Solitude.

"I don't think about whether or not I like it," he finally said. "It's just who I am. What I do."

Strange that his thoughts reflected the reverse of hers. She wondered why. "You don't differentiate between the two? The who and the what?"

He shook his head. "It's all the same in the end."

Something in his tone of voice . . ."Is that your choice?"

"What's to choose? You do what you do because you are who you are."

A warrior's sentiment. A man called. A man certain, sure. A man who stirred her blood in ways she could barely fathom. It was so unexpected yet so very real.

She shifted to face forward again, deciding she'd hold up her end of the conversation much better without his profile or the cotton-covered round of his shoulder and biceps in her vision's field.

What she didn't count on was the impact of simply having him near. Drawing a breath that wasn't scented with his clean musky warmth was impossible.

Who needed oxygen, right? She'd simply hold her breath.

"I can see that, I suppose. Since I've written one thing or another most all of my life."

He remained silent for several long moments, and it took more willpower than she'd have ever expected not to glance over. It took another whopping amount not to scoot closer to him on the long bench seat.

Finally, he spoke. "Why do you write what you write?"

"Excuse me?" She arched both brows then frowned.

"If you've always written. Always wanted to write. Why your column?"

"Ah," she mused softly, smiled softly. "You don't think gossip and lifestyle observations are real writing then?"

She felt the heat of his gaze, the change in his breathing pattern, in the car interior's temperature, in his body language as he leaned toward her rather than away—they all made his opinion perfectly clear.

"I didn't say that." His voice rumbled deep and low. Intimately low.

It was all she could do to sit still. "You didn't have to. Your silence screams your disapproval."

"It's not my place to approve or disapprove." He checked his mirrors. "I'm not your audience."

"You're right. You're not." But he had issues with her column anyway. She needed to let it go. She really did. But it bugged her to be dismissed without reason. "That's why I'm curious as to the basis of your complaint."

This time she did glance over. It was his left wrist now hooked over the steering wheel, his right arm draped along the back of the seat.

Her peripheral vision picked up the motion of his hand as he flexed his knuckles; his fingertips brushed her shirt collar. She felt the sting of his heat and stayed put.

"It wasn't a complaint," he said, looking at her, his eyes hidden behind his dark lenses. "It was a question."

"A question with an attitude," she said, her chin coming up.

"Really?" His mouth quirked. "You think so?"

"Yeah. I know so. I get it a lot." She moved her gaze back to the road ahead, then turned to stare out her passenger side window, regretting that she'd allowed him to stir her insecurities.

That she'd let him put her on the defensive was bad enough.

"So why do it?"

How the hell had he turned the tide of this conversation to wash over her like this? "Why not? I'm giving a whole lot of readers exactly what they want."

"Whether they need it or not."

"And that's your job? Determining what they need?"

"No. My job is making sure you live to write another day."

"Even though I have nothing worthwhile to say."

"I'm sure you have all sorts of worthwhile things to say."

Argh! Men! "So why am I not writing hard-hitting news pieces, you mean? Instead of fluff?"

"Putting words in my mouth now?"

She practically heard his smirk, so she glanced over; oddly enough, his expression appeared as blank as a slate. He seemed to have snatched her from the jaws of death only to bait her with this maddening conversation. "No. I'm only interpreting your comments based on my experience. You think I'm wasting my time and talent."

"That's your spin."

"And what's yours?"

"I only asked why you've chosen to write what you do."

"Because, believe it or not, I offer an escape to a lot of women."

He muttered in that strange foreign language again. "An escape from what? Bad hair days?"

She was beginning to get a sense of where he was coming from. In fact, she'd bet all the money she had on her that he'd been screwed over by a material girl. "It's a visceral thrill for some. To read about experiences they'll never know themselves."

"And that's what Peter Deacon gave you. Those experiences."

"He did, yes."

"And they were important."

"To the veracity of my column, yes."

"So you used him."

"Yes. I did." She took a deep breath and spit it out. "I purposefully and willingly used a man. I admit it. And I enjoyed it. So stuff that in whatever it is you use for a pipe and smoke it."

Julian wasn't sure why he'd badgered her for the admission except that everything he'd seen of her in action contradicted his wealth of intel.

And everything he'd seen during his stints in Egypt and Kenya made it doubly hard to overlook his instincts about women who put stock in material things. About the damage inherent to greed.

He didn't like to be wrong. He was glad to learn he hadn't been. She was exactly the high maintenance diva he'd been led to believe.

Funny then how he still wasn't convinced. How he didn't want to be convinced. How he wanted her to be different because of how much he wanted her.

At least none of his SG-5 partners were on hand to toss his uncharacteristic behavior into his face.

Julian Samms did not suffer fools lightly. Yet he was on the verge of becoming a big one because his dick had its own hardheaded agenda. "Another case of turnabout being fair play?"

"How's that?"

"He was grist for your fantasy mill, and you gave him legitimacy and . . . whatever."

"We were never lovers. I told you that."

"Knowing his reputation, that's a pretty damn hard story to buy."

"I'm not asking you to buy anything. I'm telling you the truth."

A truth he wanted to believe. The idea of Peter Deacon's hands on this woman turned Julian's stomach in inexplicable ways.

He continued on State Route 9336, driving through the entrance into Everglades National Park, glancing in his rearview mirror and breathing easier the longer the road behind them stayed clear.

"I hate to be a nuisance, but do you mind telling me how much longer till we stop?"

"Forty, forty-five minutes." Probably closer to an hour considering he wasn't driving the roadster.

"And where are we're going?"

"A safe house."

"I see. And we'll be safe there?"

"That's the idea."

"For how long?"

"Until it's safe."

She collapsed into her corner of the front seat.

Yesu. "Katrina, listen. I really don't know. I won't know until Mick checks back in. Rivers is a blockheaded shit, but he's smart. And he's dangerous."

"I know. I felt the sting of his bullets more than once."

"I'd like to get you to a clinic, get your foot stitched up. But I'm afraid if I don't get you off the street then that foot will be the least of your worries."

"You're welcome to do it yourself."

"Say what?"

"You've got sutures in your first aid kit."

"I don't think you want me to do that. Unless you don't care that your foot ends up looking like Dr. Frankenstein's baseball."

"Well, it is the ball of my foot."

He laughed. He couldn't help it. A laugh that he hoped didn't sound as desperately hysterical as it felt.

"Wow," she said, and grinned. "That was nice. You should do it more often."

"Can't. Would ruin my ruthless bastard rep."

This time Katrina was the one who laughed. "Did you earn that reputation? Or pick it out of thin air for my benefit?"

If they hadn't been traveling well over the posted speed limit, he would've slammed on the brakes, climbed between her spread legs, and shown her what a ruthless bastard could do with a bench seat.

He never should have laughed. That one slip in his armor had stirred the tension inside the car unbearably. He was already running on adrenaline and dealing with close quarters and death's snapping jaws.

He sure as hell didn't need this new intimacy. "It's for my benefit. Not yours."

"How does my thinking you a ruthless bastard benefit you?"

"Because now when I invite you into my bed you'll say no."

"Do you want me to say no?"

What he wanted was for her to take off her pants and sit in his lap while he drove. What he wanted was to take back the admission of wanting her, to regain the advantage lost with the show of weakness.

But he didn't say another word. He couldn't. Not when all the things he wanted to say and wanted to do—to her and with her—would double the trouble they were in, would blur the focus making sure he stayed sharp, would keep him up nights remembering why her type wasn't his.

Thankfully, she didn't seem much in the mood for conversation herself. She simply stared out the window while he took them another thirty-eight miles into the park. A very long, very slow-going thirty-eight miles.

The tension in the car nearly killed him. She was too close for his argument about not being his type to hold. Too strong for a woman he'd expected to be vulnerable when out of her league and her element. Too ready to give as good as she got the way he liked a woman to do.

Wo cao, he thought to himself, knowing the sentiment to be true. He was fucked. The road continued until they reached the fishing camp on Florida Bay. He circled the bait shop and the motel's office, heading for the maintenance shed behind.

"We're here."

Six

Where they were was the tip of the peninsula, deep inside Everglades National Park. The far end of nowhere. Isolated. Abandoned. Alone.

Funny how she was neither worried nor afraid when either response, both responses actually, would've been understandably appropriate.

Instead, she wanted him to answer the question she'd asked all those miles ago. Because now she could think about nothing but his invitation, whether or not it would come, if it would be a test, an assessment of her character, a challenge, or nothing more than a sexual proposition.

Mostly, she wondered what she would say if and when it did come. Right now? She really didn't know.

Once they'd left the main park road and circled behind what appeared to be a fishing camp, mangroves lined one side of the path, palms the other, creating an effective blind alley.

That was how she felt. That she was traveling forward but with no idea where she was going.

Until today, she'd been so bloody sure.

Now here came this unusual man who, with a few caustic comments, pointed questions, and offhand remarks had cut to the heart of doubts first stirred when she'd learned the truth of Peter Deacon.

"This is your safe house?" she asked as the trees gave way on one side to more prairie with Florida Bay beyond, and the structure came into view. It looked like the rundown camp's redheaded stepchild.

Ignored and forgotten and dilapidated at that.

Julian scoffed, a humorless sarcastic sound. "And here I thought you more than anyone would know not to judge a book by its cover."

His slams were beginning to get on her nerves. Or maybe it was the fact that he'd wedged up against her defenses that had her on edge.

Then again, it could have easily been the near-miss shootings responsible for her mood.

Whatever it was, she snapped. "It's hard not to in this case. My life is in danger, and those four walls don't appear capable of keeping out the wind, much less any gunshots fired my way."

He didn't even respond. He did no more than park the car, grab the first aid kit and her pool tote out of the backseat, and order her to wait. She watched him cross the dirt drive to the three front steps, unlock the door, and enter.

He obviously felt they were safe enough for her to stay in the car alone, but she still couldn't shake the sensation of being watched.

Ridiculous, she knew, because they were on the tip of nowhere. If any eyes were trained on her, they belonged to Peeping Toms of the raptor or reptilian sort—a thought that had her second-guessing her decision to get out and stretch her cramped legs.

Julian returned less than five minutes later, jogging out to open her door. She swung her right foot to the ground, propped her left on her knee, and eased the shoe back up over the bulky bandage.

The reality of her injury set in when she stepped from the car. Her foot refused to bear but the slightest bit of her weight. She pitched forward, and grabbed onto the car door for balance.

Julian stepped in and wrapped his arm around her waist. "You okay?"

"Uh, not really." The admission escaped with a panicked bit of a laugh. And a wince. "I've obviously been sitting too long."

"Judging by the lack of color in your face, I'd say it's more than that." He muttered under his breath, that weird dialect again. "Let's get you inside."

He bent then, scooped her up like she weighed no more than a feather pillow, kicked the car door shut, and carried her to the shack.

And, oh how right had he been with his reminder that appearances could be deceiving. Once through the doorway, she swore she'd just set foot inside a plush rental on any Florida vacation beach.

The interior was painted a cheery sky blue, the main room's furnishings done in shades of mango, banana, papaya, and lime, the floor in a winter white tile.

"You've got to be kidding me," she mumbled, glancing around at what was truly a cozy little cottage. "This is a safe house?"

"You were expecting industrial cinder blocks?" Julian's chest rumbled as he spoke, reminding her of their respective positions.

Not that she had forgotten so much as done her best to focus beyond his heat and his strength, his bulk and the sure beat of his heart.

Now that he'd spoken, however, it was all brought back in a sizzling frisson of awareness.

One too powerfully real and compelling to overlook.

For now, however, until she'd had time to process the scope of their situation—the intimacy, the isolation, the fact that he was here to keep her alive and nothing more—overlooking was exactly what she needed to do.

"I guess that's pretty close." She looked around again, took in the brightness, the cheeriness, the plush sofa and side chairs in a print that would pass for African tribal if not for the fact that it was done up in fruit tones rather than rich golds and browns. "I think of safe houses as being dingy and dreary."

"You've been watching too much bad spy TV."

He was probably right—though *Alias* hadn't been the same since Will Tippin's departure. "Uh, maybe you should put me down. Let the blood circulate back into my foot so I can see how bad it really is."

He grunted, carried her through the small house to the bathroom where he'd stashed the first aid kit. He lowered her to sit on the toilet seat and braced her foot in his lap once he'd sat on the edge of the tub.

From the kit he pulled sutures and an antiseptic swab, from beneath the sink a bottle of Betadine. She watched his efficient movements, mesmerized by his lack of hesitation, his certainty, his economy of motion, the wicked concern drawing down his brow.

She looked away from the distraction of his face to that of his hands. Large capable hands with deft fingers that distracted her in ways she preferred he not know. Ways totally inappropriate for the time and place and situation.

Strangely, however, the pain in her foot took away none of the pleasure of his touch. Or perhaps she was able to bear the one because of the other.

Whatever the case, it took her a moment to realize he was waiting on her.

"You ready for this?" he asked. "It's going to hurt like hell."

"I haven't been ready for anything that's happened today." She braced herself with one deep breath, curled her fingers into her palms and dug her nails deep. "This, at least, I think I can handle."

Where the hell was Savin and why hadn't he checked in? Not that Mick would've had time yet to pick up Rivers's trail, but still.

Julian wanted to hear from his partner, needed to hear from the other man, swore if he had to remain isolated for long with only Katrina for human contact he was going to go *kuang qi de.*

And he sure as hell didn't like any of what that said about the self-discipline that had been as much a part of keeping him alive as had his ability to read the people in the crowds he infiltrated.

Reading Katrina was throwing off his plans to hole up, to keep his distance, to wait for Savin to take care of Rivers, then deliver her back to her life.

Dumping the crabs he'd boiled into the sink filled with the ice he'd picked up during a quick run to the bait shop for perishables, he grumbled to himself. The sick and twisted part of this whole scenario was that reading her should make keeping his distance easier.

But the opposite was turning out to be true. He'd expected to be turned off by the woman who expended creative energy describing the details of her high-maintenance lifestyle for no reason but to feed the fantasies of others.

Instead, he was turned on by a woman who'd shed silent tears while he'd sewn up the gash in her foot.

It had nearly killed him, puncturing her already damaged skin, knowing that he was doing a shitty job because he couldn't keep his hands from shaking.

Some kind of tough guy operative he was. Letting a long tall wisp of a woman knock him sideways.

He tossed the boiled new potatoes into a bowl with salt and butter, sliced the meaty tomato he'd grabbed from the stand outside the shop, and called it dinner.

Katrina was already sitting at the table around the corner, her foot propped up in the seat of the vacant chair to her left, while she flipped through a two-year-old issue of *Florida Wildlife.*

Julian managed to get the food, plates, and utensils, a bottle of wine, and two glasses out of the kitchen in only two trips. Returning from the second, he stopped to watch her situate the place settings as if she were some sort of fucking Martha Stewart.

He dropped the bowl of potatoes with a thud. "We're not usually so formal here."

She shrugged, gave a weak smile. "Old habits. Hard to break."

He grunted. A less than human response but the only one he was capable of making, one appropriate when he considered his vow to keep his distance and his very human weakness making that a hard promise to keep.

He sat down opposite her and tossed her a red shop rag. "I couldn't find paper towels or napkins. I'll pick some up if I make another supply run before we leave."

"This is fine. More practical than wasting all that paper." She spread the rag over her lap like she would a linen napkin then forked up a tomato slice. "Do you think we'll be here long?"

"Shouldn't be. Mick's got a bloodhound nose." Why the hell couldn't she complain about something? Anything?

"Have you worked with him long?" she asked, cracking open a crab leg.

He watched the liquid run over her fingers, expected her

to wipe or lick herself clean, groaned when she did neither, when she left the juices glistening on her skin.

He cleared his throat. "Mick? Not really. He was pulled onto the team six months ago. The rest of us have been working together quite a few years."

"Is this a private organization?" She stabbed a potato, bit into the whole of it while still on her fork.

"Private?"

She nodded, chewed, and swallowed. "As in not military or law enforcement."

Wo de tian a! "What's with the twenty questions?"

She stopped eating then and met his gaze squarely, when as fierce as his frown felt, he'd expected her to flinch. He'd wanted her to flinch.

Flinching meant he still held the upper hand, the advantage, was in full control of the situation. Her lack of flinching confirmed his biggest fear of all.

As far as Katrina Flurry was concerned, his control had been shot all to hell.

"I'm making conversation, Julian. That's all."

"I don't do small talk," he said, stuffing an entire potato into his mouth so he didn't have to do talking of any kind.

She tilted her head to one side and considered him. "We could talk about something larger. Nietzsche or Chomsky or Aquinas or Spielberg."

He sputtered. "Spielberg?

"Ha." She winked, grinned. "Made you laugh."

But he wasn't laughing now. Instead, he was making up his mind whether to eat her for dinner or dessert.

Seven

"Twenty questions isn't such a bad idea, you know," Katrina insisted twenty minutes later as the food—the only real buffer between them—rapidly dwindled along with what conversation she'd managed to force.

Julian frowned, stacked the empty tomato plate on top of his, which now held nothing but a pool of melted butter. "Say again?"

"Something to do besides stare at the walls." Since he was obviously not big on talk of any size, and she didn't think he'd like her spending the rest of the night drinking him in. "The magazines aren't exactly my cuppa tea, not to mention being out of date."

He canted his head toward the living room. "There are DVDs in the bottom of the TV cabinet. No cable, so no reception, but the movies are there."

"As is the Playstation." Men and their toys. She cocked her elbow over the back of her chair. "Thanks anyway. But I'm not into video games, anime, or CGI-driven flicks."

"Don't tell me you don't dig Tolkien," he said with a disbelieving snort. "At least this new version. I thought all you women were into the long-haired, pointy-eared British elves."

She shook her head, wishing for *Pride and Prejudice* or *Bridget Jones's Diary*. "My British fantasies are all about Colin Firth. The way he walks. The way he looks into a woman's eyes."

"Sorry." Julian banged more dishes together. "We're fresh out of chick flicks and female porn."

"Don't write yourself off so blithely," she said, curiously pleased when the dishes rattled.

He growled. "What the hell is that supposed to mean?"

Strangely, she was growing rather partial to his surliness. "You cook, you clean. You sew."

When she wiggled her toes, he rolled his eyes. When she winced, he sobered. "You okay?"

She sighed, hating the feeling of being an invalid. "I will be as long as I keep the weight off and the movement to a minimum for awhile."

"Sit still. Let me get the table cleared and I'll carry you to the living room."

"Sure," she said, and nodded, waiting till he turned the corner before pushing out of her chair and hobbling into the other room on her heel.

She lowered herself slowly to the floor beside the coffee table and collapsed back against the couch.

Between the wine- and pain-induced giddiness and the attempts on her life, not to mention the fact that the man with whom she was holed up gave Colin Firth a run for his money, she was feeling rather not in her right mind. Was rather out of sorts, in fact.

Was even wondering if she might not rather sleep with Julian than sleep alone. Sleep as in closing their eyes and not saying a word. Not sleep as in hot slick bodies.

A thought that drew forth the moan she'd been holding

back since seeing Julian in that too small T-shirt in Maribel's kitchen.

Or perhaps since the chieftain/maiden fantasy she'd woven as they drove.

Whenever it had happened, she was now suffering from a mighty crush that she feared would bring on more trouble than it was worth. Which was why it would be a monstrous mistake to indulge.

Oh, but how she wanted to, to get her hands on that fabulous hard body, to cuddle up and let him protect her, soothe her, make her sweat.

"If you're not going to sit still and wait for my help, I'm not going to have a lot of sympathy for your pain."

She looked up to where Julian towered above her, his expression fierce, concerned, hard with impatience. "Oh, I'm not in pain."

One brow went up, a warrior who was certain he wasn't being given the truth. "Sounded like a moan to me."

"It was. Just not of the painful variety," was all she said. Against her better judgment, she led him on, teasing, testing the waters, ridiculously turned on when that was the last road she needed to travel.

"I see," he replied, still staring down, seeming to dare her to open her mouth and say more.

A more she wasn't sure of, that made her nervous, that left her with a hollow feeling needing to be filled.

And then he reached into his front pocket, pulled out a deck of cards, and tossed it to slide across the coffee table. "I found these in a drawer in the kitchen. Since my movies and magazines aren't up to your standards, a card game?

She sighed heavily, picked up the box, turned it end over end on the table. "What did you have in mind?"

"Poker? Blackjack?"

"Stakes?" she asked, one brow raised.

"Since I'm short on cash, it'll have to be clothes."

He was goading her and he didn't know why.

No, that wasn't true. He was goading her because he wanted to piss her off.

If he pissed her off, he'd be guaranteeing she wouldn't want a damn thing to do with him. Right now, that wasn't the case.

She'd had too much wine, was in too much pain, still had to deal with a killer.

And that was the reason—the only reason—she thought she wanted to take him to bed.

He watched her flip the box of cards on the table, from top to side to bottom to side, until it was all he could do not to snatch it out of her hand. Women did not make him nervous.

This one was driving him mad.

No. Forget mad.

He was on a fast track to certifiably insane now that she had stopped with the cards, now that she was worrying her lower lip with her tongue and her teeth, now that she was looking up at him with sleepy-lidded eyes.

"You're on," she said at last, and this time he was the one who groaned. "I'm too muzzy-headed for poker, though. I have trouble remembering the hands as it is."

"Blackjack then."

She nodded; her eyes drifted shut. "That I can probably handle."

"Forget it," he said, and turned to walk off. She wasn't even going to try. She was going to give in, let him win, get naked, and call it a night.

"And here I thought you were the type to enjoy a good challenge," she said behind his back.

If she only knew. The challenge wasn't going to be winning at cards but the end game of turning her down.

"Besides," she went on, "you haven't ever played my version of blackjack."

He turned back, stared down where she rested against the base of the couch, her head back on the cushy seat cushion, one knee drawn up, her injured foot pointing toward him.

He followed the line of her long leg from her foot up her thigh, wishing he hadn't because even in baggy men's jeans she did more for him than a woman had done in a very long time.

"Your version?"

She patted the floor at her hip. "Come sit, and I'll explain."

He tossed the red shop rag he'd used to dry his hands onto the kitchen table he hadn't finished cleaning, crossed the tiled floor, and sat.

Not beside her, though. That would be too close to tempting fate.

Instead, he kept the table between them, draped a wrist over his updrawn knee, and said, "Explain away."

"Okay. I draw two cards from the box and hand them to you. You draw two cards from the box and hand them to me."

"That's it?"

She nodded. "That's it."

"You're making this up as you go along, aren't you?"

"Actually, yes." She tilted her head to the side and considered him from beneath her long lashes, the tips of which brushed her honey blond brows. "I was trying to make it as dangerous as possible. You know. To fit with my life's current theme."

"Katrina," he growled, "what's happening here isn't a joke."

She stared for several seconds, her eyes unblinking, before she hurled the deck of cards toward his head. He caught them, raised a brow, waited.

"I know it's not a joke," she whispered, the sound a raspy sob as she pointed an index finger at his face. "But don't you dare deny me the right to deal with it however I have to. Even if my dealing doesn't follow your rule book for looking death in the face."

Elbows on the coffee table, she buried her face in her hands, her hair, free from her ponytail, falling forward like a concealing curtain. He didn't want her to cry. He sure as hell didn't want to be the cause.

He'd convinced himself she was incapable of taking anything seriously, of giving credence to anything deeper than designer labels. But one by one she was shooting the legs off the ladder he'd used to climb into his ivory tower.

He'd been casting down stones to destroy her façade when there had been no need. She wasn't who he'd thought she was at all.

Unless she was a hell of an actress and he was a big fat sap.

He flipped open the box and knocked the cards loose like he would a cigarette. "You want to pick first or you want me to?"

"You've got the deck. You go," she said, brushing back that mane of hair and looking at him with purely dry and, oh, such wicked eyes.

Sap, hell. He was a fucking puss. He slid two cards from the box, slapped them facedown on the table.

She took the box from his hand and did the same for him. He met her gaze, refusing to check out the cards he'd been dealt. "I win, I want your pants."

"Fine." Her voice didn't even shake. "I want your shirt."

She turned over her cards, the queen and ten of hearts. *"Ai ya,"* he muttered, knowing she'd have no idea who or what he was damning, and flipped his two of clubs and four of spades into the center of the table.

He muttered further while yanking his T-shirt over his head and off. He tossed it beyond her shoulder to the corner of the couch.

And he swore the moment fabric hit fabric, the mood in the room tightened to bursting. As if a ratchet had been applied to the tension and torqued.

Katrina's sleepy, seductive eyes widened, then closed. She pursed her lips, blew out a slow, steady stream of breath. A subtle shudder seized her limbs and she flexed her fingers, pointed the toes of her left foot.

It was when she looked back at his face that he knew the depth of the trouble he was in. Wine or no wine, pain or no pain, she had sex on her mind.

And not the cheap and quick, any-dick-will-do variety, but intimate and intense sex with him.

"You going to deal or what?" he finally asked, hating the raw sound of his words.

She tapped the box on the table, tugged two cards free and used two fingers to slide them to him facedown. Then she offered the box, which he took, grabbing the two topmost cards and slapping them down for her.

She picked them up, but was a long time looking at them, her gaze wandering instead over his bare shoulders and throat and what she could see of the rest of him with the table blocking her view.

Meat. *Zhandou de yi kuai rou.* He felt like a friggin' piece of meat, and forced his gaze to his hand, which was no better this time than it had been the last.

A five of hearts and six of diamonds. A whopping total of eleven.

Katrina turned her cards over slowly and one at a time. The seven of diamonds. The six of clubs. Besting him by two. *Gou shi.* Shit, shit, shit.

She stared at both hands of cards, worried her bottom lip with the edges of her teeth, finally lifted her gaze, which had grown heated and heavy, to say, "I want the band from your hair."

He blinked, caught off guard, having expected her to strip him to his skivvies. Instead, he tugged the leather band the length of his hair and handed it over, watching her watch the strands brush his shoulders, watching her watch him shove it back from his face.

He couldn't help it. He had to know. "You looking for something in particular?"

She shook her head, grinned slyly. "Just a fantasy I've been entertaining lately."

He snorted, grabbed up the box, handed her two more cards. "Here. Fantasize that this time I win."

"Okay, but you realize I have to take off my shoe to take off my pants, which is an unfair advantage."

Fuck unfair. He just wanted another look at her long bare legs—and was willing to give her even more advantage to make it happen.

"Here." He reached down and slipped off both of his shoes. "I'll give you two shoes to your one."

She didn't even hesitate, adding her athletic high-top to the mix, turning over her king and ace of spades.

He gave a cursory glance to his nine and jack of the same friggin' suit and reached for his fly.

"Wait."

Hands at his waist, he looked up.

"You're still wearing two socks." She made a "gimme" motion with her hand. "One of them will do."

For her, maybe. He was ready to be done with this exercise in bad luck that was dragging out way too long. He wanted to get to sleep because he was not going to bed her.

Still, he did no more than pull off one sock as she picked up the deck of cards.

Finally. He stared at his two tens while watching her turn over two fours. Once he laid his cards down atop hers, she reached for the copper button at her waist, lifted her hips, tugged the denim down and off.

That left her sitting in borrowed white panties that did little to curb his appetite.

They played another round without speaking. Not that either of them had said much at all—a reality that should have made him a lot more comfortable than it did.

Mindless, uninvolved sex he could handle. If he took her right now, that was exactly what he could have. He could get her out of his system and be done with it.

But that wasn't what he wanted. And because he wanted more, he wasn't going to allow himself to do more than look and lust.

He lost his second sock and they played again. This time when he won, he couldn't even gloat because he had no idea what to ask for.

The way she sat now, the elastic legs of the panties teased his line of vision. He could see the edge of one hip before his view was blocked by the bulk of the table.

Taking her panties made less sense than her top, her bra, her one sock, or even the diamonds twinkling in the lobes of her ears.

And so because he was half bastard, half gentleman, he asked for her bra.

"Interesting choice," she said, smiling as she reached beneath her loose shirttails for the back clasp. "Rather safe, yet rather sexy."

"Just working with my own fantasy over here," he said, figuring it was a safe enough admission.

"You intrigue me, Julian Samms. I thought you'd go for the instant gratification of getting me out of my panties."

"Nope." He shook his head, watched her breasts bounce

beneath the white oxford cloth, and swallowed hard. "Never been the gratuitous sort."

A smile played over her lips as she reached for the cards. A smile that had him wanting to respond in kind. And to kiss her. And to slit his own wrists for both.

"Whose turn is it?" she asked.

"Does it matter?"

"I suppose not. Since neither of us has much left to lose."

"Really?" he asked perversely, feeling angry and frustrated for no reasons that made sense. Having no one to blame but himself. Wishing they were anywhere else and there for any other reason than the threat on her life. "Nothing much to lose?"

"I'm talking about clothes, Julian," she said, canting her head to one side and weighing him curiously. "That's all."

He didn't say anything, but took the cards she dealt him before choosing two for her. He lost, and waited for no more than the lift of her eyebrow before skinning down his pants.

"Will you do something for me?" she asked as he slid, depending on his luck, what could very well be the game's last two cards across the table. "Will you come to bed with me tonight?"

She turned over the hand she'd been dealt. His knocked them out of the park. Her shirt or her panties. He was clueless on how to decide. "We're not going to have sex, Katrina. Not tonight."

"That's okay," she said, smiling as he showed her his cards. "I just don't feel like sleeping alone. Not tonight. Not after today."

She waited for him to respond, but his throat had swelled to the point that he couldn't even swallow. He thought of holding her close for no other reason than that of her needing him.

It was a thought that left him stunned and with nothing to say but, "Go to bed, Katrina. I'll be in soon."

He got to his feet, helped her to hers, looked away as she limped her way around him in nothing but a shirt that was too sheer and borrowed panties that shouldn't have been the least bit provocative.

He didn't look back until he had no choice. Then and only then did he watch the hem of her shirt flirt with the curves of her bottom, take in the length of her legs, her slender ankles, the way her slow progress never drew a single word of complaint.

Once she'd closed the door to the bedroom, he grabbed up the cards, shoved them back into the box, and returned them to the kitchen where he stood staring at the floor.

In the dark it was so much easier to picture Kenya, and to wonder why the visual memory of the blood he'd spilled—and especially the why—was doing nothing to help him keep Katrina at a distance.

How the hell he was going to get through this mission, he hadn't a clue. He wasn't even sure he was going to make it through the night.

Eight

Katrina lay curled on her side unsleeping, waiting, wondering about the strange game of blackjack she and Julian had played hours ago. Wondering what the hell they'd been doing besides making a bad situation even worse.

Wondering how a game of cards could so obviously be not about winning or losing at all.

She punched her pillow into an even harder knot beneath her head, pulled her knees closer to her chest, winced when she jabbed the toes of her good foot into the ball of the other, elevated on a spare pillow.

Having sat still for Julian's needle earlier, she swore now that she'd make the worst field soldier ever. Focusing on his warrior's face was the only way she'd gotten through the pain.

She had nothing on which to base this visceral attraction. Yes, he was gorgeous, but so had been Peter Deacon. And she better than most knew looks had nothing to do with who a person was.

What Julian's appearance did, however—because it was

more than the set of his mouth, nose, ears and eyes—was compel her to discover what about him left her feeling as if she would never, even with her best years ahead, have time enough to learn all there was about him to know.

He was enigmatic, aggravating, and arrogant. But he was also kind. Very very kind. And funny whether or not he wanted to be. He was serious as the situation demanded, and vigilant, and formidable.

Such simple qualities proved what a good man he was. One more complicated than all the men she'd known combined.

Her eyes were already closed when the bedroom door opened, but still she squinted at the soft spill of light from the lamp left on in the other room. Julian closed the door just as quickly as he'd opened it and stepped to the far side of the queen-size bed.

She realized she was holding her breath, listening for his movements, his bare footsteps on the tiled floor, his discarded clothes rustling. What she wasn't expecting was the heavy sigh he expelled. Or how her heart raced at the feel of his weight settling at her back.

She moved nary a muscle, waiting for him to speak, to fall asleep, to shift closer or farther away. He did none of that. He did nothing at all.

And so she finally turned onto her back and gave a sigh to match his. "I'm not asleep."

"I know." His voice rumbled through the coils of the mattress.

She felt the vibration the length of her spine and curled five of her toes. "Too much on my mind, I guess."

"Your foot?"

She shook her head. "It throbs a bit, but I just took more Advil."

"You've got it propped up on a pillow still, yes?"

She smiled to herself. "Yes, boss."

He grunted.

This time she laughed. "It's okay. I'm so out of my element here I need direction. Even of the bossy sort."

He said her name with a growl. "Then listen to me when I say the one thing you need now is sleep."

"I know. I just can't." Her mind was a jumble of so many thoughts, zipping here, there, everywhere. Coming back always to him. "I need more wine. Or a really good orgasm."

He nearly broke the bed frame turning from his back to his side. "No sex. My rules."

"Oh, I don't need you for an orgasm," she said, digging her own grave even deeper. "And I wasn't suggesting sex. Simply thinking of effective sleep aids."

"Jesus," it almost sounded like he hissed, draping an arm over her middle and hauling himself close. His breath was warm where it stirred her hair when he muttered, "Go to sleep, Katrina."

That might happen if she were to be hit on the head with falling debris.

"I can't." Not with the way he'd surrounded her, his arm, so heavy and warm, the bulk of his body, his face so close to hers. He suddenly seemed much more threatening than any assassin's bullet.

A threat she feared would turn her life as she knew it upside down. "I'm sorry. I just can't."

"You're starting to piss me off here, woman."

Such sweet talk from the man she was falling for. "A bedtime story would be nice. Or even twenty questions."

After a short silence, he said, "Ten."

"Ten?"

"Ten questions. Not twenty." He moved so that his chest pressed her shoulder. "And hurry up before I fall asleep."

She felt as if he'd given her the moon. She also felt as if his skin would set hers on fire.

"Okay, number one." *Think, think, think.* What did she

want to know most of all? "Have you ever been, are you now, or will you soon be married?"

"That's three questions," he grumbled.

"Only if it requires three answers."

"Still making up rules as you go along?"

She would've smacked him but wasn't sure he wouldn't smack back. "Answer, please."

"No, no, and no. Three answers to three questions."

She didn't care what he said. She was only counting it as one. Then again, the wealth of information gained was worth letting him keep score.

Now for the nitty-gritty. "Does what you do for a living ever scare you?"

He responded with a snort. "All the time."

"Do you make a lot of money?"

"Scads. Stop being shallow. You just wasted number five of the ten."

She smiled to herself. "I was just trying to figure out why you do it if it frightens you."

"It's more of an adrenaline buzz than true fright." He paused to adjust his pillow. "Besides, being scared is no reason not to do what you know is right."

Finally. That peek into his psyche she was wanting. "Do you always know what you're doing is right?"

"Does this count as one of your questions?"

She considered only for a moment because this one mattered more than the others. "Yes."

"I wouldn't do it if I didn't know it was."

"Is that why you came after me?" she asked softly.

"Yes. And that's seven."

She allowed a private smile, then sobered. "Do you know why Peter's firm would want me killed?"

"Yes," he said, then said nothing more.

"Are you going to tell me?"

"That wasn't what you asked."

True. She'd only asked if he knew. She felt as if she were wasting her questions, though she was quite sure he wouldn't hold her to the original ten. Not when she had so much at stake and when he didn't have it in him to be that unfair or unfeeling.

She twisted her fingers into the top edge of the sheet. "Why, then? It's not like Peter shared anything about who he was. I don't pose a threat of any sort."

"They seem to think you do. That he leaked information. Or stored it in your place."

"He was never in my place." He'd been arm candy of the cosmopolitan sort. Not her lover. "He did a lot of business in Miami and kept a suite at the Mandarin Oriental. I would meet him in the lobby when we went out."

"I don't need to know the details, Katrina."

"But I want you to know." *Nice. Now she sounded like a shrew.* "I don't want you to think less of me because of lies you've been told about my relationship with him."

"This is a job. It doesn't matter what I think."

"It matters to me." She shoved his arm away, used the heels of her palms to scoot herself up in the bed to a sitting position. "I'm not the bimbo flake you've obviously determined that I am."

"And that bothers you."

"Yes, it bothers me." She was used to being judged by her appearance, by what she wrote, which was often deemed fluff. She wanted Julian to see the truth. "It bothers me a lot."

"Why?" he asked, flopping onto his back.

She was not going to cry. She was not going to cry. "Because I don't want you to feel like you're wasting your time saving my life."

He cursed in that strange foreign language and squirreled around roughly to sit on the edge of the bed. "Don't put that bullshit about one life being worth more than another into my mouth."

His words reverberated in the small room, bouncing from wall to wall like a ping-pong ball. She dodged the impact; the move was too late. The bitterness with which he'd loaded the statement slammed her back.

He hurt. He ached. He lived and breathed a pain unlike any that had hurt her as a child.

She'd lost track of how many questions she'd asked him. It didn't matter; there was only one thing left she needed to know. Had to know.

The only truth that mattered.

"Julian?"

"What?" he snapped, his breathing harsh.

"Who did you kill?"

Of course he hadn't answered her. He'd done what she'd expected him to do. He'd left the bed, cursing violently—or so she assumed—and left the room.

Following him would've been the wrong thing to do. That much she hadn't needed a crystal ball to see.

So palpable was his anger, in fact, she wouldn't have been surprised had it taken the form of a sentient being. The emotion was that obvious, that very real.

What she didn't know was whether she was the cause. Or if her question had simply tugged on the roots of an event time had long since grown over.

Either way, keeping the width of the cottage between them for the time being had seemed a safe course to stay.

Eventually, she'd slept. Or so she assumed since a pale gray light now limned the shade covering the window above the bed. He'd had long enough to cool off, long enough to brood and to stew.

It was time he got over himself, time he let her in. She wanted her answer, especially considering that after the coast was clear and she got back what remained of her life, she wasn't going to want to let him go.

That much she knew for a fact.

Wearing nothing but the dress shirt she'd had on now for eighteen hours, she slipped from the bed and eased out of the room. The front of the cottage was dark but for a wedge of light casting an eerie glow from the kitchen.

The refrigerator. She'd bet her bottom dollar.

She limped her way around the corner, took in the view awaiting her, and froze. Julian stood in the triangle of the open door, staring at the meager contents, wearing nothing but long-legged boxer briefs.

Oh, for a thousand words.

Seeing the body that had been in bed with her earlier took her breath away. The shoulders and chest, which were broad without bulk. The abdomen, which was flat yet rippled. Long arms, large hands. The leanly muscled legs of a triathlete. The thick package of his sex above.

She didn't want him to know she was there. Ridiculous when he'd probably sensed her stepping from the bed.

Still, he never said a word. And she never moved. Even when he looked up to see her half naked and staring.

He closed the refrigerator door then, silencing the room's grating light and returning the intimate darkness. She heard her own harsh breathing over the quiet, heard his, too, above his footsteps on the linoleum floor.

The rhythm of their heartbeats charged the air in the room, a deep throbbing beat older than man's soul. A powerful, telling beat that spoke of hunger and fear, of life and survival, of love and desperation.

When he reached her, he slipped his hands beneath her shirt, circled her rib cage, lifted her to sit on the countertop,

and wedged himself between her legs. He trailed his fingertips over the plump sides of her bare breasts before going to
work on the shirt's buttons.

Her hands found their way to his shoulders, her legs
around his waist. He kept his gaze trained on his fingers
until he reached the last button in the row, the one closing
the shirt tails between her legs.

Only then did he look up, the meager light glinting off
the blue in his eyes.

The shirt fell open; he spread his palms over her thighs
and said in a voice she barely heard for his gruffness, "If
you want to stop me, this is the time."

"I don't," she whispered, and shook her head. She didn't
want to stop him at all.

Nine

Her surrender stripped away what remained of his damaged control. He slept with women he met on the job. Never with women who were the job.

And this was why.

From this moment on the stakes were higher for both of them. He couldn't afford to split his focus. But neither could he afford the price of walking away.

He slid his hands from her thighs, up over her hips and rib cage, his thumbs teasing the outer curves of her breasts until he reached her shoulders.

Once there, he spread open the two sides of the shirt and bared her skin to his gaze. The light wasn't enough to see more than the glitter of the diamonds in her earlobes and her shadowed form, but that was okay.

He saw all he needed to see with his hands. Her softness, her firmness, the gooseflesh on her upper arms, the cold sweat of her nerves.

He thought about soothing her with the words women loved to hear. How he would never hurt her, how she couldn't be any more beautiful, how he wanted her beyond what he'd known possible.

He didn't say any of that because none of it mattered. The lies overshadowed the truth. He would hurt her in the end. That much he knew to be fact.

And right now was all about loving her body with his.

She sat unmoving, her hands on his shoulders, her heels in the small of his back, her chin lifted, her long neck exposed. He wanted to be everywhere at once, to touch and to lick and to fuck.

He started by taking her shirt all the way off and pinning her wrists to her hips. He liked the idea of immobilizing her; he didn't know why. He also liked how close her breasts were to his mouth, the way she smelled of sunscreen and the sweat of the day.

It was a sexy smell, natural, real. He leaned in, his face between her breasts, and ran his tongue from her sternum to the base of her throat where her pulse beat and her moan of pleasure rumbled.

When he lifted his head, she struggled to free her hands and tightened her thighs where she gripped him. He chuckled against her skin, enjoyed her resulting whimper, then moved to the left and took her nipple into his mouth.

She tasted salty and sweet and he wanted to see her, to know if she was the color of an apricot or a plum. He suckled and tugged, and her low throaty cries tugged at him in return. He felt the pull deep between his legs, felt the blood surge until he thought the head of his cock would explode.

Christ, but this wasn't supposed to happen so fast. This need to bury himself inside of her, to feel the tight walls of her beautiful cunt squeeze him and milk him and drain him until he ran dry.

He moved to her other breast, nipped and licked and sucked and did his best to pretend he was doing so with a nameless, faceless body. One he would enjoy and pleasure but would never see again.

Not one belonging to a woman whose life was in his hands.

He pulled away, let loose a flurry of curses he knew she wouldn't understand. Yet it wasn't until she said, "Julian?" in a voice so soft he melted with it that he admitted to the gravity of this mistake.

And then he did what he had to do.

He kissed her.

He let her arms go, and she wrapped them around his neck, kissing him back like staying alive depended on how well she used her teeth and her tongue.

She used them like a courtesan, a high-paid call girl, yet he knew the intensity of the kiss was real. Whether fueled by lust or driven by fear, her response was genuine and the hottest thing he'd ever known.

He slid his tongue deep into her mouth, seeking to deepen her fire along with his own response. He held her face in his hands, sweeping through her mouth, tasting her, moving closer so that her breasts flattened against the muscles of his chest.

The sounds she made were of heat and hunger, and he growled in return, filling her mouth with all the words he couldn't say, with passion unfamiliar and raw and consuming.

She cupped the back of his head, pressed her thumbs into the tired muscles at the base of his skull, massaged him there as she pulled her mouth free to kiss his face, his eyelids, the skin beneath his neck.

Enough, he barked to himself, undeserving of her tenderness when this was only sex, not emotion, not feeling, not involvement. It had to be so little. He couldn't trust it to be more.

He pulled free, took his frustration lower, nipping and licking his way from the hollow of her throat down her body, tonguing her navel, spreading her thighs wide with his hands and breathing in the scent of her sex.

She shuddered. From no more than the heat of his breath, she shuddered. Her reaction had him pins-and-needles impatient to witness her come. To feel her pussy contract around his cock, his fingers, his tongue.

He started with the latter, kissing his way up her thighs, left to right, holding her ankles as she leaned back on her elbows, until he reached the soft crease where her leg met her sex.

He tongued her then, licking his way between her swollen lips and finding her clit. She cried out when he drew on the knot with his lips and sucked, a sound of pain mixed with pleasure that had his balls drawing close to his body, his cock surging up to the sky.

He lifted her legs, draped them over his shoulders, and skinned out of his briefs before ringing his fingers around the base of his shaft. He squeezed his cock with one hand, used the thumb of the other to pull back the hood of her clit.

He exposed her to the air and to his mouth, circling the nerve endings with the tip of his tongue until her hips left the countertop and she raised up towards him.

She offered herself fully, and he took the gift, slipping one finger then two inside of her, sucking on the lips of her pussy, her clit, and stroking himself as he did.

He was dangerously close to unloading all over the cabinets and floor. She did that to him, spun him off the axis that had kept him stable since Hank salvaged his sorry wind- and sunburned ass from Kenya all those years ago.

He'd spent the time since embroiled in his work, banging who he could when he could. But nothing had prepared him for this.

He released his cock, slid his free hand up her body to cup a breast, to slowly pinch his fingertips around one nipple. She lay all the way back then, covered his hand where he tweaked her, sent her other hand down between her legs.

She tangled her fingers with his, masturbated, slipping her thumb into her cunt to pleasure herself. He couldn't believe it. Could not believe this woman.

He swirled his tongue in and out and around, wedged her thighs wider apart, pulled her other hand away from her breast and urged her to play.

She snugged two knuckles around her clit, rubbed and tugged and thrust up against him. He slid the flat of his free index finger beneath her pussy, pressing against the entrance to her ass.

She was sobbing now, her head thrashing, begging him to take her, to fill her. He wet his finger with her juices and did, sliding into her slowly as she clenched around him.

She came then, and he'd never seen anything like it. Never known a woman so uninhibited, so open, so explosive. So much a part of her own experience. Convulsions tore through her; she contracted around both their fingers. Pre-cum beaded on the tip of his cock.

He tried to ease her down slowly, but his own ass was aching from the tightness, the swelling. Sweat ran down the middle of his back as he held his body in check.

But she didn't want to be eased and gentled. She wanted more, telling him so with a gruff, "Move," as she shoved him back with the sole of her good foot planted in the center of his chest.

He stumbled, she jumped down, turned, and bent over. He thought he was going to die. Thought he had when she gruffly whispered, "Julian, please, fuck me."

He cursed, jerked open the kitchen drawer of twine and scissors and electrical tape, searching out the condoms he knew were there.

Once he was sheathed, he took hold of her hips and stepped into her body, sliding himself between her thighs, knowing if he used either of the entrances to her body she offered, he'd be done like a Sunday pot roast.

He breathed deeply, smelled her musk, and hardened further, taking time to wrap a mental fist around his flyaway control.

"Do it. Please. Do it now."

"Let's go to bed. Get you off your foot."

"My foot's fine. Other parts of me are in desperate need of attention. So attend, already."

Though nothing about this was funny, he chuckled. And then he surged forward into her sex, which was wet and hot and amazingly still tight. He pumped as hard as he could, slamming into her.

All the while she cried, "Yes," and "More," and "Harder. Fuck me harder."

It was over almost before it began. He felt the heat of his load burst and turn him inside out. He squeezed the muscles around his ass, dipping his knees to drive into her, realizing that her fingers were buried in the folds of her sex as she brought herself off once again.

He waited through her cries and contractions then pulled free, spun her around, and ground his mouth to hers, kissing her thoroughly until they were both satisfied. And neither one of them could separate his taste from hers.

Ten

She wanted him again. Already. She ached and burned and knew she was torn and raw. It didn't matter. She had to have him again and now.

First things first, however. Taking hold of his hand, she led him through the front room, now bathed in dawn's sunlight, down the hall, through the bedroom, to the bath.

"Wait a sec," he said, disappearing only to return seconds later with a roll of duct tape and two food storage bags.

"You need to keep the stitches dry." He ordered her to sit on the toilet lid while he sat on the tub's edge and took her foot in his lap, slipping both bags over her injury, taping the tops tight to her ankle.

It was a surreal scene, sitting there naked, neither of them acknowledging what had just happened, the organic intensity, the mind-blowing way they'd so thoroughly taken one other apart.

She wondered if he thought less of her because she wasn't the least bit proper when it came to enjoying sex. She tilted her head to the side, studied his face as he concentrated on the task at hand. "I didn't mean to shock you."

"Shock me?" he asked, never looking up.

Fine. Make her spell it out. "The sex."

"The sex we weren't supposed to have?"

"That would be it." The man was a master of avoidance. "Did I? Shock you?"

"Does it matter?"

She jerked her bagged foot from his thigh. "Yes. It matters a lot what you think of me."

He looked at her then, his expression the same one he'd been wearing since she'd met him. The one that made her nuts because she couldn't read him at all.

So she wasn't the least bit surprised when he asked her, "Why?"

She got to her feet, leaned behind him to start the water running in the tub. "For the same reason that I wanted you to know that I never slept with Peter. Because as much as I love sex"—water temperature adjusted, she straightened, stood, looked him in the eye—"I tend to have most of my sex alone. I don't indulge with any man who asks. Only with a man who I can't imagine not having. One who turns on my mind as well as my body."

She swore a pleased smile flittered across his stoic face as he got to his feet. "The best sex always begins in the mind, Katrina. Trust me. There are still a few of us Neanderthal types who know that."

She didn't know what to say. She'd expected him to clam up again, not give her this glimpse of the man he was beneath his warrior's façade. Speechless, yet certain she was grinning like a fool, she stepped into the tub, thankful for the nonslip strips on the bottom, and pulled the lever for the shower.

Julian followed, closing the curtain, handing her a bottle

of shampoo. She met his unwavering gaze as she leaned back and wet her hair.

"You know what I would love?" she asked, working up a head of lather as she backed up beyond the showerhead to give Julian access to the spray.

He wet his head and body and came up sputtering. "What's that?"

"Clean clothes. If I'd known we were going to have to hole up in the middle of the Everglades, I'd've packed appropriately while we were at Maribel's."

"Actually, we have clothes here."

His long dark hair reminded her of Johnny Depp in *Chocolat*, Daniel Day-Lewis as the last Mohican, and she couldn't help but blow out a long slow breath. "What sort of clothes?"

He poured a puddle of shampoo into his palms. "T-shirts and sweats. And, unfortunately, nothing in your size."

"I don't care." She nudged him into reverse, flattening her palm in the center of his impressive chest, moving beneath the water to rinse her hair once he was out of her way.

That done, she planted her hands at his waist and danced around him in the narrow space. "Anything soft and cotton sounds like heaven. Those jeans were beginning to chafe."

"I thought you looked pretty damn hot in those jeans with your ponytail swinging," he said, eyes screwed up as he rinsed shampoo suds from his hair.

She caught a quart of water before she managed to close her dropped jaw. "Julian Samms. Are you actually flirting with me?"

He shrugged, reached for the plastic bottle of body wash he'd left on the back of the commode. "Doesn't seem too out of line considering where I've had my hands and mouth."

She felt a blush rise from her toes to the roots of her hair. "I suppose you have a point."

He glanced down. "Nope. Not right now. I'm still pretty soft."

She was not going to rise to his bait, no matter that her heart tingled with his teasing. "Brain sex, huh?"

"Best sex organ in the body."

Hmm. She cast her gaze toward his groin, the thatch of dark hair there where his thick—but soft—penis nestled. "You're right, of course. Though don't discount the other organs you do have."

"I never do."

"And I'm sure all the other women whose lives you've saved have appreciated it as well."

He opened his eyes then, stared down and demanded her attention with no more than the sharpness of his gaze. "I don't sleep with women I'm assigned to. You're the first. And I plan for you to be the last."

She swallowed hard, knowing what he wasn't saying. He wasn't saying that he'd never sleep with another woman. Only that he'd made a mistake sleeping with her. A mistake he wouldn't make again.

What she wasn't as sure of was how she felt about what was an obvious truth.

She tried to casually toss it off. "So, this thing we're doing here is like those commercials? What happens in Vegas stays in Vegas?"

He nodded. "It can't be any other way."

She sighed. "I guess I thought . . ."

"What? That this was something emotional? Or real? More than an affirmation of life and all that?"

He was right, but it still hurt like hell to hear him say it. After all, he wasn't the one who'd made the mistake of falling in love. "Why me, then? If you don't sleep with the women you're paid to protect, why me?"

"I'm not paid to protect women, Katrina. Not anymore."

She started to write off his comment as semantics but

was stopped by the look in his eyes. A look that had her wanting to ask when he'd stopped, why he'd stopped.

A look that reminded her he'd last walked out when she'd questioned him about who he had killed.

She'd bet her last nickel it had been a woman whose well-being had been in his hands. And she wasn't quite sure how that made her feel.

"Okay then. Forget the paid protection. Why me?"

He arched one of those dark warrior's brows. "Because you make it hard to say no."

She sputtered. "That's about the lamest thing I've heard come out of your mouth. And it doesn't tell me a thing."

The brow lowered. Lowered more, deepened into a deadly-looking crease. "You want the truth?"

Why did his tone of voice make her want to tremble, to run, to hide? "The truth is always a good place to start."

"Because you're not who I expected you to be," he said simply.

"Back to that, are we?" she asked, her ire rising along with the shower's steam. "Pretty girl who writes fluff can't possibly have any redeeming qualities?"

A stream of unfamiliar words rolled from his tongue. "Katrina. For christ's sake. You wear diamond earrings to sunbathe."

She closed her eyes, opened them again, set her jaw, and reached for the stud in her left earlobe. Then she grabbed Julian's hand and dropped the earring into his palm. "There. Feel better now?"

"I don't want your fucking diamonds," he said, handing it back.

She slapped at his hand. The earring fell, skittered across the tub and down the drain. It was like watching her connection to Peter and the disaster of the last few months wash away.

She couldn't believe the uplifting sense of relief. She reached for the other. "I don't want them either."

Julian snagged both of her wrists, pinned them to the wall on either side of her head. "Stop it."

"Stop what? Stop doing what I have to do to save my own life? Isn't that why we're here?" She shivered from his heat and his fury, and finally saw herself in his eyes. God, she'd been so stupid not to see it before. "Or is your perception of me as high maintenance giving you a problem with that?"

"You don't know shit about what you're saying, Katrina," he growled down.

She lifted her chin, feeling as if her heart would rumble straight out of her chest. "No? Then why don't you explain it."

"Why don't I just fuck you instead," he said, a nanosecond before his mouth came down.

He tasted like raw anger and unleashed rage, and none of it frightened her at all. This was who he was, a bottle of emotion needing to explode.

And so she let him, matching every stroke of his tongue, every nip of his teeth, every harshly inhaled breath, yet being the cognizant one, the one to finally ease the kiss back from a disastrous precipice.

She struggled against the hold he had on her wrists, demanding he relent. When he refused, her demands became insistent.

She pulled harder, slipping her hands from the vise of his; he flattened his palms against the wall on either side of her head while she wrapped her arms around his waist and pulled his body close.

She angled her head, pushing up into the kiss, feeling the tremors that gripped his body, surprise that he'd revealed himself so, thrilled that he trusted her that much.

She soothed him with her mouth and with her hands, sliding her palms over the hard straps of muscle on either side of his spine, massaging him with her fingertips, the heels of her palms, drawing on his lips with tiny sucking kisses.

He was huge and threatening as he loomed above her, his stance, his bulk, his fierce internal fight that she knew he didn't want her to see. She didn't have to see a thing. She felt and tasted it all, and when he shuddered and gave up one sharp sound that was almost a sob, she swore she fell completely in love with every inch of this damaged warrior.

Her warrior. Her man.

Moving his hands to cup her face, he softened the kiss. She was so glad they were where they were so the tears welling and falling from her lower lids vanished into the water drops beaded on her face.

Whatever he'd seen, whatever he'd done, it was killing him, yet nothing she could say right now would mean a thing because he was a man and he understood the language of sexual intimacy more than he did words.

And so she used her body, her hands, and her mouth, pulling away from his kiss to trail tiny love nips over his throat and collarbone, down the center of his chest to his belly.

He didn't even move. He remained statue still, rock hard and aloof, his hands coming to rest on her shoulders as she pushed back the shower curtain, turned to sit on the edge of the tub, and took his growing erection into her mouth.

He was soft and hard and thick when she took him to the back of her throat, cupping one hand to hold his sac, wrapping her other fingers around the base of his shaft.

She stroked him as she sucked him, the moisture of her mouth and that from the shower creating a slick lubrication, one she used to explore the extension of his arousal where the hard ridge rose behind his balls.

He muttered beneath his breath, sharp foreign words that had her smiling, had him asking, "What's so funny?"

"That language. What is it?" she asked, and went back to circling her tongue around the plum-ripe head of his cock. Oh, but she loved his taste.

"Mandarin."

She grinned again. "As in oranges?"

"As in Chinese. Christ, Katrina. Don't make me talk."

The idea that she could make him do anything thrilled her. And suddenly she didn't want to do this anymore. She was selfish and she wanted more. Wanted the fulfillment of having him inside of her.

With her lips pursed around his tip, she looked up and met his fiery gaze. "Julian?"

He growled.

"Would you make love to me now?"

The words were barely out of her mouth before he reached for her, hooking his hands into her armpits and pulling her to her feet.

His face was set in an expression of hopeful determination, and she smiled at the thought that she'd put it there. But that was all the time she had to think because his mouth was on hers again, his hands on the backs of her thighs lifting her up.

He pinned her to the wall with his weight and drove into her. She tore her mouth from his and cried out, wrapping her arms around his neck and holding on for the ride.

It was fast and furious, his erection stretching her open, his fingers gouging into her skin. She loved it all, the need, the power, the shattered control.

Her sex burned and ached with the friction and the arousal spreading through her like swamp fire, insidiously taking hold until putting it out seemed an impossible task. She would never get enough of this man.

She felt the flex of his legs on the backs of her thighs as

he primed himself to come. His pleasure kindled hers unbearably, and she buried her face in his neck and let go.

He followed, and the sounds of their shared pleasure closed around them in the cloud of steam, wrapping their joined bodies in an embrace that felt like forever.

Eleven

SG-5 Safe House, Saturday, 9:30 A.M.

Julian held Katrina close in bed, listening for her deep even breathing before gathering up the courage to say what needed to be said.

Earlier they'd finished showering in cold water, then tumbled between the sheets afterward, using one another's bodies for warmth.

At least that's how it had started, a teasing and tickling case of Katrina's shivers, and his selfish intentions to get his hands on her under the guise of rubbing the circulation back into her skin.

But the need for warmth had quickly turned into the need for much, much more. For one another and solidarity and so many things that weren't about the situation they were in at all but were about the two of them as a man and a woman.

He'd made love to her again, the way he'd wanted to from the very start. Slowly. Looking down into her eyes, her breasts pressed flat beneath his chest, her ankles crossed in the small of his back.

He ground himself against her, rotated his hips in slow motion, watched tears leak silently from the corners of her eyes as she'd come.

He was exhausted. And she was finally asleep. But he wanted to tell her the truth.

He wanted her to know who and what he was because the small hold he still had on hope was growing tighter and stronger the more time he spent in her company.

And if there was even the remotest possibility this was more than sex, she had to know everything. Details he'd told no one. Details none of his SG-5 partners nor even Hank Smithson knew.

Spooning up into Katrina's body, Julian wrapped his arm around her middle, tucked her head beneath his chin and breathed deeply. "I was in Kenya when it happened. Assigned to a task force that no one digging through military records would ever find. We didn't exist, but we knew that going in."

He stopped, waited to see if his whispered words had disturbed her sleep, or if he was safe to go on. Her hair, which tickled his nose, smelled like the sea, like fresh air and freedom, and he lay there for long moments and did nothing but breathe her in.

"We were guarding a family of tribal royals from Burundi who were in negotiations to use the port at Mombasa. They wanted access to the facilities they would need to export their coffee beans. We were only there to make sure the meetings happened. No one wanted to see more civil unrest hit the news. Not after Rwanda."

What happened had been more like the chaotic urgency of Somalia and *Black Hawk Down* in the end. But the beginning was the killer. The decision he'd made causing all hell to break loose. The one he would have to live with every day for the rest of his life.

"It happened at zero three hundred," he said, then realized he should back up to make the whole thing clear for her. And for his own piece of mind.

"The wife of the tribal leader never appeared in public without wearing every piece of gold she owned. She knew exactly how dangerous it was but was too arrogant to care. I hated that bitch. She was bad news from day one."

Which was why he'd taken her on as his personal project. He'd been determined she wouldn't fuck up an assignment that should've been as simple as a baby-sitting job.

"It was the last night before they crossed the border and our services would no longer be needed. They refused to stay in any of the villages where shelter had been offered, so we pitched tents every night. And we traveled at a snail's pace because the elders couldn't handle anything more."

He stopped because he needed to breathe. He swore he hadn't talked so much at one time in years. He liked privacy. He liked silence. He liked sticking to the business at hand. Getting in, getting it done, and getting the fuck out.

He sure as hell did not like spilling his guts. But then, that's what had started this all, wasn't it?

"It was the middle of the night. I heard a struggle and a muffled scream inside her tent. One thing she had made sure I understood was that she never entertained overnight guests." He huffed his disgust. "She had also made sure I knew I was the exception.

"At first I thought the noises were a ploy to get me inside. She was like that. Manipulative. Entitled. But when I went in to check it out, I saw it was nothing like that at all."

He was suddenly cold, and pressed his thighs closer to the backside of Katrina's, wrapped his chest around her body, seeking comfort, a sensation so unfamiliar he almost couldn't breathe because of the way it raced through him.

"She was holding a kid, threatening him with a knife

that would've scared the shit out of a butcher. He was probably ten or twelve but looked like six. And he had his hands wrapped around a dozen of her bracelets."

Even now he heard the woman's words, heard her cold orders. *Kill him. Kill this thief now or I will gut him and leave him as carrion for the scavengers. And then I will do the same thing to you.*

She would have done it. And suffered no consequences. In an ugly twist of fate and foreign policy, the camp of tents was considered a mobile embassy, the inhabitants subject to diplomatic immunity.

That didn't mean he'd been able to let her.

He'd looked into the child's eyes and seen desperation, but nothing even resembling fear. Nothing resembling hope. Whether he died of a knife wound, a bullet, starvation, or disease, he would die. And he knew it.

"I took him out," Julian whispered, and choked. "Had one of my men help me dig his grave. And then I shot him because it was the right thing to do. I turned myself into my superiors after that. The end of my military career."

And the beginning of another once Hank Smithson had gotten wind of what had gone down.

Julian turned onto his back then, flung his forearm over his eyes and waited for the sweats to begin. For the aftershock of reliving that night that had defined his life. Of having to live with himself since.

But they didn't come. And his heart didn't throttle like an outboard motor. Neither did his muscles seize up and burn. Even when, at his side, Katrina stirred.

"I didn't know they grew coffee in Burundi," she said softly, turning over on the mattress and into his arms, drifting in and out and only hearing part of what he'd said.

And that was okay. She didn't have to hear it all. It was enough that she'd responded to his voice. That she was here.

He held her closer than he'd ever held another woman in

all of his life. And he didn't even flinch when she whispered, "I love you."

The words settled into his skin and soothed instead of stinging like he'd braced himself for them to do for years. It was a ray of hope strong enough to slash across his darkness, and it made him smile.

It was midafternoon when Katrina finally woke for the day. Had she been at home, she would have headed to the gym, where she would sweat and ponder her column due on Monday.

As it was, she was pretty much assured she'd never have a deadline again.

Strangely, that didn't bother her at all. Not after the incredible twenty-four hours she'd just come through. She was aware now like she hadn't been before how little what she did for a living mattered. Or how being alive was nothing compared to feeling alive.

Escaping a killer's bullet had helped her make the distinction.

Falling in love with Julian Samms had defined the differences in the subtlest of ways.

She pushed up and swung her legs over the side of the bed, surprised to find the flow of blood into her foot hurt less than she'd expected. Surprised, as well—and pleased—to find a clean white T-shirt, socks, and gray athletic sweats on the foot of the bed.

She hobbled her way to the bathroom and did her thing, glad to find the borrowed panties she'd hand-washed last night dry enough to wear. She dressed and exited ten minutes later to find a steaming cup of black coffee on top of the bedroom's dresser. *Oh, wow,* she thought, smiling like a crazy woman to herself.

What she didn't find was any sign of Julian, though she swore she heard him talking. And swore his voice was coming out of the bedroom wall. Coffee in hand, she stepped across the room and slid open the door to the closet.

The interior wall was actually a panel that hid a tiny hutch of a room where Julian sat in front of an electronic console, a set of headphones held to one ear.

He glanced her way, held up a finger signaling her to wait. She nodded, stood in the entrance, studied the bank of high-tech equipment that was like nothing she'd ever seen.

No, that wasn't true. She had seen one similar. In a movie. On the command deck of a spaceship.

And that's when it finally hit her. The truth about Julian Samms. Who he was, who he worked for. It was all so far and above anything she would ever understand. A truth she would probably never fully know or even grasp if he told her. Told her . . .

What was it that he'd told her during the night?

She frowned as she sipped her coffee, certain she'd heard his voice, picked up random words, though she'd never surfaced to grasp what it was he was saying.

What she had latched onto was the feeling in his tone, the emotion behind the confession. Yes, confession. She was sure that's what it had been.

And looking at him now, even with the fierce expression casting shadows over his face, she sensed that his spirits had lifted.

Whatever it was that had happened beyond the incredible sex, she was glad she'd been there for him.

"Right," he finally said, adding, "I'll be in touch," before dropping the headphones to the surface of the desk, where he propped his elbows before burying his face in his hands.

She moved closer, ducking beneath the low-hanging entrance to place her palm on his shoulder. "Are you okay?"

He swiveled his chair toward her, grabbed her by the hips, and pulled her between his spread legs. When he lifted his gaze, she braced herself, one hundred percent certain she wasn't going to like what he had to say.

"Mick's been shot."

"What?" Her heart bolted to the base of her throat. "Who?"

"Rivers."

"Where is he now?" she asked, not even sure which man she meant.

Julian didn't wait for her to clarify. "Mick's safe. He'll be fine. But Rivers is on the loose."

Twelve

Katrina didn't know what to say. Knowing what to say depended on knowing how to feel.

How she felt was numb.

Or at least that was her initial reaction. Moments later the reality set in along with the cold sweats and the nausea.

Her stomach burned and heaved. Her throat ached. Her foot throbbed.

She'd been expecting to be a free woman in another few hours. Maybe a day. Maybe two.

As long as she'd known Julian's partner was on her shooter's trail and she was in capable hands, she'd been able to convince herself she'd be out of harm's way soon. Back to Miami. Back to her life.

Now, however, she was able to convince herself of only one thing. She was going to be sick.

She bolted for the bathroom and dropped to her knees. Her coffee cup slid from the counter where she'd set it into the sink with a clatter. Eyes closed, she grabbed for her hair, and that was it.

What she'd swallowed of the coffee came up along with remnants of last night's crab dinner. She retched, heaved, and spit her way through the process of her stomach turning inside out.

Humiliation blazed—she didn't want him to see her like this—overshadowed only by an angry fear. How dare these people ruin her life when she was only an innocent bystander?

Minutes later, Julian was on the edge of the tub at her side with a wet cloth. She lowered the toilet seat and flushed, collapsed back against the wall where she let him bathe her face, thinking that no man had ever done this for her.

That there had never been one she had wanted to. One she would have allowed to.

"Thanks," she said, taking the rag and opening it up over her face. Hiding behind it and wishing for a magic toothbrush to appear.

"I can make you some tea," he suggested tentatively. "Some toast."

She nodded, smiling, pulling the cloth away. "Tea and toast would be nice. Thank you."

He shrugged one broad shoulder. "Sounded like a girly sort of thing to offer."

She smacked him across the shin with the wet cloth for being such a man. "Are you calling me a girly-girl?"

"Get over it. I like you that way." Hands on his knees, he got to his feet. But he stopped before leaving the room. "I do like you, you know."

"I should hope so," she said, because flirting was easier and healthier than panic. And because flirting with Julian felt right in ways she'd either forgotten or never had known.

"Katrina, I'm not going to let him get to you."

She stared up into his gorgeous eyes, eyes brimming with an emotion he couldn't hide. Tears welled and spilled from her own in response.

And this time it was the fear of losing the man she loved to a killer's bullet that had her hugging the commode.

The front door had opened and closed before Julian registered that the sound had come from the other room and not from the toaster behind him.

He was in the kitchen scavenging for a pink or blue packet of artificial sweetener, and had decided Katrina would have to settle for sugar in her tea when he heard her go out.

Unless what he had heard was someone else coming in. *Tzao gao.* Shit. He didn't figure Rivers for that dumb. Katrina on the other hand . . . and his SIG was hanging on his chair in the comm room.

He dashed through the house, snagged up his holster, slipped it on, and hurriedly reversed direction, hitting the outside steps in time to see her top half disappear behind the car's open back door.

She scooted out, turned to sit on the bench seat as he jogged down the steps toward her. He swore she was going to fry what was left of his patience. "What the hell are you doing? Trying to get us both killed?"

Her gaze came up sharply. Hurt at first, then mad. "I only wanted the house shoes." She had her hands wrapped around the fuzzy pink slippers she'd brought with her from Maribel's house. "I'm about to kill myself in those bulky sneakers."

He reached in and grabbed her upper arm, forcing her out of the car. "You don't leave the house, understood? You want something from the car? You tell me."

She jerked away, opened her mouth to obviously give him an earful, never got out a word. The car window shattered all over the both of them.

Julian shoved her back, dove into the car on top of her. He went for his gun; she grunted as his elbow caught her solar plexus. Then she scrambled into the floor behind the driver's side seat before he could say a word.

At least a word in English, yelling, *"Liukoushui de biaozi he houzi de ben erzi,"* just as the rear windshield exploded. Glass pellets burst inward. Katrina screamed and covered her head.

Her forearms took the brunt of the blast. Blood peppered her skin where she was hit. She whimpered softly but didn't move, didn't speak, didn't even breathe.

He needed to draw Rivers away from the car, away from Katrina. He bailed into the front seat, kicked open the passenger side door. He pressed his head back into the headrest, counted to ten.

"Rivers! We need to talk."

He turned to glance over the seat at Katrina—just as Benny answered with a single red dot of his laser sight on Julian's white T-shirt. He ducked, but it was too late.

The shot came through the driver's side window, lifted him off the seat, and slammed him to the ground. The last thing he heard before darkness took him was Katrina's scream.

And Benny Rivers's hollow laugh.

Julian came to to searing light in his eyes, searing heat swarming over his body, and searing fucking pain ripping his shoulder apart.

He squinted, grunted, winced, and unscrambled what he could of his brain. Rivers. The gunshot. Katrina. *Qingwa cao de liumang.* He struggled up to his good elbow . . . only to realize he wasn't wearing his shirt or his holster.

And that he wasn't alone.

Crouched on the ground beside him was a man packing supplies into Julian's first aid kit. He blinked, focused, stirred to the fact that he'd been wrapped up and taped up and put back together again.

Just like Humpty Dumpty.

He cleared his dry throat. "How bad is it?"

"You were two inches away from needing your shoulder rebuilt." The man, his dark skin glistening like coffee beans in the sun, zipped up the canvas pack. "That'll hold you until you get to a hospital."

Julian shook his head. "No hospital. I've got to go . . . somewhere."

"Then I hope to hell you have another way to get there." Squatting now, his wrists dangling over his knees, the man nodded toward the borrowed car. "Rivers did a number on your spark plug wires."

Julian turned his head slowly to take in the other pieces of the V8 engine strewn on the ground like so much litter.

He had to find Katrina. With Mick out of commission and the trail gone cold . . . He needed to get inside, raise Kelly John or Christian. There had to be word on the wires about Rivers.

Rivers . . .

Pushing to sit upright, Julian turned back to his visitor and sized up the other man who knew way too much about Katrina's assassin.

His reflective sunglasses and combat boots, weathered skin-and-bones appearance, his dreads tied back in a black bandanna, and the Tac-Ops Tango 51 slung across his back—it all said one thing.

Julian had just hit a big fat dead end. A roadblock worse than any he'd erected to keep those who tried to get close at a distance. His partners. Hank.

Katrina.

Didn't matter much now. He wasn't going to have much of a life left once this man was through with him. Though why he'd patched him up first . . .

Julian frowned, said, "You're Spectra."

The man nodded, stood, shook a dark cigarette from the

thin square box he pulled from the pocket of his black T-shirt. He offered one to Julian before firing up the lighter he dug from a webbed pouch on the leg of his khakis.

He drew smoke into his lungs and blew out a long slow stream, then stepped back and kicked Julian's SIG across the drive.

"Hell of a situation here, isn't it?" he said, bringing the cigarette to his lips again.

The hell? Julian stared at the gun as if seeing a mirage before picking it up, scooting back against the car, holding his injured arm close to his body.

His palm scraped over gravel and broken glass, but his gaze never left the other man's face. And his hand never left the gun. Even though it had been freely given.

Spectra was just as good at taking away. "Do you know where he is? Where he took her?"

From another pouch pocket, the agent pulled a GPS locator. "Looks like they're back in Miami, man."

Christ! He'd been out that long? "What do you want?"

"Me?" The man shrugged. "I want Rivers."

Julian levered himself to his feet using the sedan's door frame. "What're you doing here then? If you want Benny?"

"I figured you might want the girl." He filled his lungs one last time then flicked the cig to the driveway and ground out the fire with his boot heel. He then picked up the first aid kit and nodded toward the house. "You wouldn't have a beer in there, would you?"

Julian nodded because he was hurting too bad to think straight. He needed a whole lot of answers but couldn't come up with a single coherent question.

Holding the elbow of his busted-up arm with his good hand, he made his way to the front steps, wondering what the other man knew of where he was and who he was tangling with. Wondering if at this point either of them cared.

After all, they were about to share a beer.

"There's a six-pack in the fridge." Julian indicated the kitchen. "I'm just gonna . . . get another shirt."

Gritting his teeth as he hurried down the hall to the bedroom, he grabbed a T-shirt from the closet, stepped into the communications room, and as quickly as he could with one hand, typed the security code to launch the program he needed.

Another few seconds of using only his index finger to hunt and peck out his message to the SG-5 ops center, and he was done. He secured and shut down the system, secured and backed out of the room—right into the cold beer bottle the Spectra agent held out for him.

Having hooked the earpiece of his sunglasses over his T-shirt's neckband, the other man inclined his head toward the concealing door now sliding shut. "Nice setup."

"Yeah. It's not too shabby." Julian took the beer, and led the way back to the front of the house once he heard the click of the lock on the comm room door.

With a loud grunt, he lowered himself slowly to the sofa's edge and struggled into the shirt, sweat running from what seemed like every freaking pore on his body. He'd forgotten the pain of the gunshot.

He didn't like remembering. "You've got a tracking device on Rivers, right?"

"Actually no." The agent sat across from Julian. "It's on your girl."

"Katrina?" His pulse raced against his fast-tracking thoughts. No wonder they'd never been able to shake Benny. But how . . .

His head came up. "The earrings."

A knowing nod. "Deacon wanted to keep her in line. Who'd've figured they'd come in so handy, eh?"

Nothing here was making sense. "Why the hit on her?"

"Hell, man. There's no hit on her. That's all Rivers's paranoia." The man sat forward again, spun his beer bottle back and forth on the coffee table. "He did a lot of off the books work for Deacon. Stuff the bosses are interested in."

"And he's taking out Katrina before she can talk." *Ta ma de hun dan.* He wasn't going to let that happen. He was not going to lose this woman now.

"Not if I get to him first, my man."

Julian pushed to his feet and met the other man's gaze directly. "You know she doesn't know a thing."

"Yeah." A nod, another cigarette worked between two fingers. "She's been on the radar for awhile. Bosses know she's clean."

That was good. That was good. But it wasn't enough. He needed to make this one thing crystal fucking clear. "You so much as look at her the wrong way after this and I'll shove that rifle barrel up your ass and shoot you myself."

"I'll just bet you would," the agent said as he stood, his dangerously soft laughter rising with him, though never reaching his eyes.

Weird or not, he was Julian's best hope for getting out of here and getting to Katrina. "What're you driving?"

"Ah, my man. A Baja Outlaw." He winked. "Docked in the marina. We can blast around to Key Largo and up to Biscayne Bay."

Julian nodded, figuring how much time he needed to get out of the house, down to the docks, into the water. Calculating the equation on his way to the door, he punched the resulting instructions into the electronic keypad above the deadbolt.

This place had been the main source for monitoring Spectra IT's Caribbean activities for years now. But not anymore. Not after being compromised. He walked out, grimacing with every step as he followed the agent to the docks.

They were well into Florida Bay headed east when the

explosion rumbled around them, shooting a fireball like a rocket into the sky.

He saw the reflection in the lenses of the other man's sunglasses, accepted the silent but smiling salute as the agent touched a finger to his forehead before throttling up. And as he did, Julian caught a glimpse of the ring on his finger.

A ring worn only by graduates of the United States Naval Academy.

Thirteen

South Miami, Saturday, 9:30 P.M.

Katrina sat on her balcony's rough pebbled surface, the sharp edges biting through her sweatpants into her butt, her hands tied to the railing behind her, her foot throbbing like the head of a child's squeeze toy, while inside, Benny Rivers trashed every room in her house.

Her split lip tasted like blood and still ached from where he had backhanded her hours ago. Eyes closed, she banged her head against the iron bars behind her because her position didn't allow that she kick herself in the ass for ever getting involved with Peter Deacon in the first place.

At least she finally knew why she was going to die. It made the idea of ending this very bad weekend with a trip to the afterlife easier to take. Okay. That was a lie. She was scared shitless but had no more tears to cry. She'd cried them all out over Julian.

Or so she'd thought . . . but here they came again. Oh God. Huge tears running unchecked in rivers down her cheeks, soaking the neckband of her T-shirt, which had only just started to dry. She saw him lying on the ground, blood pooling dark and thick and red around him.

How could anything hurt this badly? So very very badly. Losing the man she wanted in her life before she'd had a chance to know him. Or to tell him. *Dear God,* she sobbed, her stomach so tightly wound she had to fight the burn of the nausea threatening to double her over. What must her mother have gone through when her father had died?

She stopped her self-induced concussion and stared up at the stars, thinking of what a hero her father had been, how he'd come to her rescue all those times when she'd been threatened with disfigurement by the girls who didn't want her hanging around their boyfriends. Or ignored by the teams who wouldn't choose her to play because girls who looked like she did couldn't throw a ball.

She missed her father so very much. She missed her mother, too, and couldn't believe she would never see her again. Would never have a chance to say good-bye. And now her mother would have to hear about what happened from halfway around the world. This was all so incredibly unfair. So very wrong.

She flinched at the sound of more glass breaking inside. She'd always loved the privacy her condo's balcony offered, how she was able to enjoy her evenings out here, unwinding with a cold drink and a good book, but right now she wished she lived anywhere else.

Closing her eyes, she did her best to put the horror of the present from her mind and think back to the cottage, imagine living there with Julian. Loving there with Julian.

Until meeting him, she had never believed anything more than attraction happened at first sight. Now she knew the truth. How two souls destined to share their lives knew it the moment they met.

And in that second, with that thought, at the very meeting of the two, her eyes flew open, her stomach quit aching, her mind began to spin.

She had to get free. She had to get back to the safe house. She had to find Julian. See for herself if he truly was dead, or whether he was still lying on the ground, abandoned, alone, and waiting for help.

The thought of him injured and helpless. Hanging on. Hoping. She had to get to him. She refused to sit here and go quietly into that good night without seeing for herself that he wasn't alive.

She had to get loose, get to her gun, and rattled the rails behind her. "Hey, Benny. Come here, will you? I need to talk to you."

A minute later, the short bulky man loomed over her in the open sliding glass doorway. "You better be ready to say something I want to hear."

She nodded, didn't even have to fake the tremors in her voice. "Peter gave me a flash card. He told me to keep it safe. I think it's what you want."

Benny snorted. "And you're just now remembering it? I don't think so, sister. This sounds like some sort of game to me."

"It's not a game. I swear." But it was. A game of playing for time. Of dealing hands of lies. Of dodging and feinting and rebounding from more of his heavy-handed blows. She swallowed hard, knowing what was coming. "I carry it in my wallet."

He stared down at her as if processing what she'd said, then turned to look inside. "I've turned this place over and haven't seen a wallet anywhere."

She swallowed again and braced herself, wondering if it would be a fist or a foot, praying for neither. His insults were so much easier to take. "It's not here. I left it back at the motel."

His head swiveled back slowly, like a piece of heavy equipment operating in slow motion. And then he reached into his pocket, pulled out his handkerchief, and gagged her. "Now why the hell would you do something that stupid? No, don't answer. Let me tell you. You're a stupid female. Damn breeding bitch."

He kicked out with all the strength of his bull-in-a-china-shop bulk behind the blow. She cowered, cringed, but it didn't do a bit of good. He aimed the toe of his shoe at the ball of her bandaged foot, and she swore she felt every one of Julian's stitches split open.

She screamed, the sounds absorbed and muffled by the fabric ball in her mouth. She willed the nausea down while working to dislodge the gag with her tongue. Choking to death was not part of the plan.

The click of Benny's knife had her screwing her eyes all the way shut and doubling over. Instead of stabbing her in the back, however, he reached down and sliced through her bonds before jerking her to her feet.

She stumbled inside, hopping on one foot, dragging the other behind her like some nursery rhyme sheep. Mary? Bo Peep? She couldn't remember. And the fact that she'd tried to spoke to her state of mind.

Looking around at the devastation of her things, she leaned her weight against her sliced and shredded sofa, rubbing the circulation back into her wrists, unable to care about anything beyond getting away.

Benny slid the patio door closed and charged into the room. She glanced quickly away from the hutch on that same wall, thankful that he didn't seem to have found the hiding place where she kept her handgun.

He grabbed her upper arm and shoved her forward so hard she nearly stumbled to her knees. "Let's go."

She tried to talk around the handkerchief, ask him to let her change her clothes, go to the bathroom, wash her face—

anything to put him off from leaving before she could get her hands on her gun. But all that came out of her mouth were gagging, muffled sounds.

"Yeah, yeah. You keep talking," he said, dragging her down the tiled foyer toward the door. "And I'll keep enjoying not listening to your fat trap of a mouth."

He pulled open the door and jolted to a stop, brought up short by the gun barrel inches from his face. Katrina's heart thundered in her chest.

"Going somewhere, Benny?" asked the dark-skinned man holding the very big handgun with the futuristic laser sight and extra long silencer on the end. "Or should I say, going somewhere without me?"

Benny jerked her in front of his body like a shield, his meaty hands wrapped around both of her wrists where he held them in the small of her back. "Get the hell out of here, Ezra. This is between me and her."

"Wrong, Rivers," said another voice from the hallway, a smoothly rough voice Katrina would've recognized anywhere, one that had her knees shaking to bear her weight. "This is between me and you."

She cried out with joy and sagged against Benny's hold as Julian stepped around the corner. He was pale, his shirt matted with wet and dried blood, his mouth bracketed by lines of what had to be excruciating pain.

But he was alive, and she cried again. Relief, fright, hope. She couldn't define any emotion but love.

"Let her go, Rivers," Julian demanded, never meeting her gaze. "It's over."

"The hell it is." Benny hefted her up as best he could— she was four inches taller and not giving him any help—and lugged her dead weight back the way he'd come, pressing the tip of his knife blade to the base of her throat as incentive.

Her eyes went wide with the sting of the prick. She felt

the warmth of the blood trickling over her skin, grimaced as Benny tightened his hold and growled in her ear. "Walk, bitch. I'll cut you open to your gullet if you don't."

He backed her into the wall beside the balcony exit and stopped, breathing hotly into her ear as he ordered, "Open the goddamn door."

She reached around his bulk and slid the door open, her gaze locked on Julian where he stood in the foyer's shadows.

Ezra had moved into the living room, his gun aimed at Benny, the red dot of the laser hitting Katrina in the eyes as Benny jerked her around. "The girl isn't part of this, Rivers. You know that. You fucked up. Peter found out. Now you have to deal."

"Forget it, Ezra," Benny yelled, the knife slacking, his voice cracking once as it did.

That was enough for Katrina. She reached for the edge of the hutch as if needing the support, flicked the switch hidden under the center molding, and held her breath as the lock on the sliding drawer released.

She felt the pull of Julian's gaze then, and looked over to see the subtle, imploring shake of his head. He could beg. He could demand. It didn't matter.

She wouldn't survive Benny's knife or the fall from the balcony to the ground. She knew she would be facing one or the other once he dragged her out the door. She had to do what she had to do to save her own life.

She took a deep breath, counted to three, drove her elbow into Benny's midsection. He grunted, loosened his hold. She grabbed for her weapon, swung it down behind her, and fired.

His howl of pain and rage took the roof off the room. She dove for the floor. Ezra fired. Benny went all the way down. And then Julian was there on his knees, helping her pull the gag from her mouth.

"Oh, God. Oh, God. You're alive." She touched his hair, his face, his neck and chest and hands. All the places she could get to while avoiding his gun-shot shoulder. "I thought he killed you. I thought you were dead." Her voice was a wet soggy mess. "I just found you and I thought you were already dead."

His big broad hand came up to cup her nape. He pressed his forehead to hers. "Shh, Katrina, sweetheart. I'm here. I'm fine. I love you."

"Oh my God, Julian!" She bawled because she couldn't do anything else. Her chest ached and her throat burned and her mouth would barely work around the words she'd been holding back far too long already. "I love you, too."

"Yeah. I know that part," he said, and she couldn't decide whether to kiss him once or kiss him forever.

And so she kissed him twice, holding him tightly as they helped one another back to their feet.

"How did you get here? What happened at the safe house? And who is he?" Arms around Julian's waist, she nodded toward the mysterious Ezra. "Should we call the cops?"

"No cops. I'll take care of it," Julian said, and she didn't need to know anything more.

Stuffing portable equipment of the medical sort back into his copious pockets, Ezra got to his feet from where he'd been kneeling next to the unconscious Benny, checking vitals, tying tourniquets, saving her would-be killer's life.

He dusted his hands together, straightened the bandana wrapped around his dreads. "You wouldn't happen to have a wheeled duffel big enough, would you?"

He wanted her help with Rivers? The sound that came out of her mouth was half gasp, half laugh. "For him?"

"Yeah." Ezra shrugged as if he were discussing a bale of hay. "I can carry him out of here, but getting him down the dock and into the boat might be more tricky."

She didn't care. She wanted him gone. "I don't have a duffel but I do have a bicycle trailer."

Julian turned to her. "You do?"

She nodded. "I even have a bike to go with it. They're in my storage unit." When both men stared at her silently, expectantly, she shrugged. "I'll get the key."

She hurried to the kitchen, grabbed the key from the hooked plaque inside the pantry door. It was when she turned to go back that she found Julian blocking her path.

"Who *is* that man?"

Julian reached up, stroked her hair back from her face. "He saved my life. And he's going to take Rivers out of here. That's all that matters."

It wasn't all that mattered. She wanted to know. Needed to know. But the details could wait.

She reached up and kissed him, gently telling him with her lips how much she loved him, and how exquisitely happy she was that he was alive.

"Now *that* is what matters," she said once she'd kissed him thoroughly, grinning as he removed her other earring, his eyes twinkling as he did. "Okay, okay. That, too."

He hooked his good elbow around her neck; she wrapped both arms around his waist, never wanting to let him out of her reach again. They headed back to the living room where Ezra had trussed Benny like a rodeo calf with a cabled rope he'd pulled out of his magic pants.

He grabbed hold of a section he'd left for a handle and dragged his load to the door. She nodded at Julian when he glanced down, then stepped back and crossed her arms over her chest.

She waited while he talked to the other man, watched while he walked him to the door. He left Ezra there with a salute and a pat on the back, and, as she watched, dropped her spare earring deep into one of Ezra's pockets.

Epilogue

South Miami, Sunday, 4:30 A.M.

"I'm really a much better housekeeper than this," Katrina said hours later, cocooned in her bedroom quilt on top of her mattress, which looked like it had suffered the wrath of a crazed saber-toothed cat.

Once Ezra had dragged Benny out the door, she and Julian had put what they could of her bath and bed to rights. They'd cleaned up together, doctoring cuts, changing dressings—her foot, his shoulder, which was in much worse shape, but for which he refused to see a doctor—checking wounds for infection, downing antibiotics from the life-saving first aid kit he never went anywhere without.

Having her hands on him then as well as now meant as much—if not more—than being alive for him to get his hands on her. She loved being alive to feel his skin, the tremor of weakness he'd tried to hide, the way he had finally and truly relaxed for the first time since she'd known him.

She laughed at that, realizing that she'd known him for less than forty-eight hours, when it felt like he'd been part of her life since the day she'd been born. Well, not quite that long, she admitted, admitting as well that she wasn't ready to give up the dramatic giddiness. Delaying a return to reality as long as possible held immense appeal.

"What day does Maribel come anyway?" Facing her, Julian snuggled deeper into the covers. "This place is a dump."

"Oh, thanks." She started to tickle him, stopped because she sensed how much pain he was in, and stroked her hand down his chest instead, threading her fingers through the dark silky hair that swirled there. "I'll call her later and see about getting your car back."

"Okay."

"Uh, and check into replacing hers?"

He nodded, stroked the hand of his good arm over the curve of the breast he could reach until she shivered all the way to her toes. "I'll take care of it. Business write-off and all that."

She would've glared at him, but his eyes were closed, making it a waste of good pique on her part. Besides, he was fairly mellow—a situation she doubted would come around again any time soon considering how he was always so "on"—and she wasn't above using his down time to pry.

"Julian?"

"Katrina?"

"Thank you."

"For?"

"Saving my life," she whispered.

His fingers, resting on the mattress, teased her navel. "All part of the job, ma'am."

"I know," she said, not even sure she could put what she was feeling into words. "But I hate thinking that you went above and beyond because of me."

His hand stopped moving at all then. His lashes fluttered; his lids opened slowly. The look in his eyes, even in her barely lighted bedroom, could never be mistaken for anything but what it was.

Julian Samms was mad. "What the hell are you talking about?"

She drew her own fists close between her breasts. "Just that I wasn't thinking. When I went out to the car. Or, I was thinking, but only about my foot. Not about our situation. I had gotten so wrapped up in what we'd done"—she couldn't believe it; she was blushing—"that for that one moment, I didn't even stop to consider the where and the why of being with you."

It was several seconds before he answered. Several seconds during which she feared confessing her alarming lack of vigilance would be the death of the very fantasy—*Julian and Katrina sitting in the tree, k-i-s-s-i-n-g*—that had been the impetus for the destruction all around them.

When he did speak, however, his words, but especially the emotion behind them, were not at all what she'd expected to hear.

"I know," he whispered, his voice rough, rife with a sense of failure. "I'd gotten sidetracked, too."

She blinked; how could he think he had failed? "You were?"

And it was then that she realized he wasn't mad at her at all. He was mad at himself. And his sigh, when it came, was heavy with it. "I heard you go out the door and wanted to kick my own ass. Not for letting you distract me, but for *being* distracted because I knew better. I *know* better."

Uh-oh, she thought, tingles of alarm centered in the small of her back.

Julian went on. "But later, on the ride back with Ezra, I realized it wasn't the fact that I'd let down my guard that was eating at me. It was the reason *why* that I couldn't get over. The same reason I'm here now."

"Which is?" she asked, almost unable to turn the words boiling in her throat into sounds. *Please, please, please, God. Don't let him go.*

"This isn't easy for me, Katrina," he said, taking a deep breath. "Admitting that I'm not enough by myself. That being on my own isn't how I want to live. That I need someone else with me."

Oh, God. Oh, God. She didn't know what to think. What to say. How to respond. Especially when she swore she couldn't tell if he was the one with misty eyes or if she just wasn't seeing things straight.

She didn't think she'd seen anything straight since meeting him. But she didn't care. Not if it meant having him in her life forever.

"Would that someone be me?" she finally squeaked out.

He nodded.

"Because you love me?"

He grinned. "Yeah. And admitting that's the easiest thing I've done in awhile."

She couldn't help it. She giggled. "Then say it again."

"Sit in my lap first," he said, shifting his hips to prod her with his penis, which had grown erect.

She shook her head. "Don't even think about it, mister. You're hurt."

He rolled over onto his back, wincing as he gave her full access. "I'll be hurting more if you don't."

And only because she wanted him so very very much, loved him so very very much, did she follow his instructions to the letter, deciding she could get used to being ordered around if it meant giving them both this much pleasure.

Eyes closed, Julian pulled in a hiss of a breath as she settled over him. The tendons in his neck stood out in sharp relief with his strain for control. "Don't move. Don't even think about it. Just sit there like a good woman for a minute or two or forever."

Male chauvinist man that she loved. Oh, but he felt so good when he filled her. When he loved her. Though, sitting still was probably just as hard on her. "I sit here much longer, we could starve, you know."

His eyes flew open. The grin that spread over his face was the final straw in securing her heart.

"Oh no, we won't." He patted the mattress above his head with one palm, searching for the pillows and slipping his hand beneath.

He rattled what sounded like plastic, way too pleased with himself as he found the secret stash he was looking for. "Here ya go."

And then of all the things he could have done, he fed her a chocolate chip cookie.

Meet the men of the Smithson Group—five spies whose best work is done in the field and between the sheets. Smart, built, trained to do everything well—and that's everything—they're the guys you want on your side of the bed. Go deep undercover? No problem. Take out the bad guys? Done. Play by the rules? I don't think so. Indulge a woman's every fantasy? Happy to please, ma'am. Fall in love? Hey, even a secret agent's got his weak spots . . .

Bad boys. Good spies. Unforgettable lovers.

Episode One:
THE BANE AFFAIR
by
Alison Kent

"Smart, funny, exciting, touching, and *hot*."—
Cherry Adair

"Fast, dangerous, sexy."—Shannon McKenna

Get started with Christian Bane, SG–5

Christian Bane is a man of few words, so when he talks, people listen. One of the Smithson Group's elite force, Christian's also the walking wounded, haunted by his past. Something about being betrayed by a woman, then left to die in a Thai prison by the notorious crime syndicate Spectra IT gives a guy demons. But now, Spectra has made a secret deal with a top scientist to crack a governmental encryption technology, and Christian has his orders: Pose as Spectra boss Peter Deacon. Going deep undercover as the slick womanizer will be tough for Christian. Getting cozy with the scientist's beautiful goddaughter, Natasha, to get information won't be. But the closer he gets to Natasha, the harder it gets to deceive her. She's so alluring, so trusting, so completely unexpected he suspects someone's been giving out faulty intel. If Natasha isn't the criminal he was led to believe, they're both being played for fools. Now, with Spectra closing in, Christian's best chance for survival is to confront his demons and trust the only one he can . . . Natasha.

Available from Brava in October 2004.

Episode Two:
THE SHAUGHNESSEY ACCORD
by
Alison Kent

Get hot and bothered with Tripp Shaughnessey, SG–5

When someone screams Tripp Shaughnessey's name, it's usually a woman in the throes of passion or one who's just caught him with his hand in the proverbial cookie jar. Sometimes it's both. Tripp is sarcastic, fun-loving, and funny, with a habit of seducing every woman he says hello to. But the one who really gets him hot and bothered is Glory Brighton, the curvaceous owner of his favorite sandwich shop. The nonstop banter between Glory and Tripp has been leading up to a full-body kiss in the back storeroom. And that's just where they are when all hell breaks loose. Glory's past includes some very bad men connected to Spectra, men convinced she may have important intel hidden in her place. Now, with the shop under siege, and gunmen holding customers hostage, Tripp shows Glory his true colors: He's no sweet, rumpled "engineer" from the Smithson Group, but a well-trained, hard-core covert op whose easygoing rep is about to be put to the test . . .

Available from Brava in November 2004.

Episode Three:
THE SAMMS AGENDA
by
Alison Kent

Get down and dirty with Julian Samms, SG–5

From his piercing blue eyes to his commanding presence, everything about Julian Samms says all-business and no bull. He expects a lot from his team—some say too much. But that's how you keep people alive, by running things smooth, clean, and quick. Under Julian's watch, that's how it plays. Except today. The mission was straightforward: Extract Katrina Flurry, ex-girlfriend of deposed Spectra frontman Peter Deacon, from her Miami condo before a hit man can silence her for good. But things didn't go according to plan, and Julian's suddenly on the run with a woman who gives new meaning to high maintenance. Stuck in a cheap motel with a force of nature who seems determined to get them killed, Julian can't believe his luck. Katrina is infuriating, unpredictable, adorable, and possibly the most exciting, sexy woman he's ever met. A woman who makes Julian want to forget his playbook and go wild, spending hours in bed. And on the off-chance that they don't get out alive, Julian's new live-for-today motto is starting right now . . .

Available from Brava in December 2004.

Episode Four:
THE BEACH ALIBI
by
Alison Kent

Get deep undercover with Kelly John Beach, SG–5

Kelly John Beach is the go-to guy known for covering all the bases and moving in the shadows like a ghost. But now, the ultimate spy is in big trouble: during his last mission, he was caught breaking into a Spectra IT high-rise on one of their video surveillance cameras. The SG–5 team has to make an alternate tape fast, one that proves K.J. was elsewhere at the time of the break-in. The plan is simple: Someone from Smithson will pose as K.J.'s lover, and SG–5's strategically placed cameras will record their every intimate, erotic encounter in elevators, restaurant hallways, and other daring forums. But Kelly John never expects that "alibi" to come in the form of Emma Webster, the sexy coworker who has starred in so many of his not-for-prime-time fantasies. Getting his hands—and anything else he can—on Emma under the guise of work is a dream come true. Deceiving the good-hearted, trusting woman isn't. And when Spectra realizes that the way to K.J. is through Emma, the spy is ready to come in from the cold, and show her how far he'll go to protect the woman he loves . . .

Available from Brava in January 2005.

Episode Five:
THE MCKENZIE ARTIFACT
by
Alison Kent

Get what you came for with Eli McKenzie, SG–5

Five months ago, SG–5 operative Eli McKenzie was in deep cover in Mexico, infiltrating a Spectra ring that kidnaps young girls and sells them into a life beyond imagining. Not being able to move on the Spectra scum right away was torture for the tough-but-compassionate superspy. But that wasn't the only problem—someone on the inside was slowly poisoning Eli, clouding his judgment and forcing him to make an abrupt trip back to the Smithson Group's headquarters to heal. Now, Eli's ready to return . . . with a vengeance. It seems his quick departure left a private investigator named Stella Banks in some hot water. Spectra operatives have nabbed the nosy Stella and are awaiting word on how to handle her disposal. Eli knows the only way to save her life and his is to reveal himself to Stella and get her to trust him. Seeing the way Stella takes care of the frightened girls melts Eli's armor, and soon, they find that the best way to survive this brutal assignment is to steal time in each other's arms. It's a bliss Eli's intent on keeping, no matter what he has to do to protect it. Because Eli McKenzie has unfinished business with Spectra—and with the woman who has renewed his heart—this is one man who always finishes what he starts . . .

Available from Brava in February 2005.

Please sample other books
in this wonderful series:
Available right now—
THE BANE AFFAIR

Christian watched the road rush by beneath the car, the roar in his ears much more than that of the engine or the tires. He should have trusted his instincts earlier. Susan's turning green wasn't about the amount of alcohol left in her system at all.

He held out his right hand, gripped the steering wheel with his left. "Hand me your phone."

"Why?"

"The phone, Natasha." He didn't have time to argue. Didn't have time to explain. Had time to do nothing but react. An exit loomed to the right. He downshifted to slow the car and swerved across two lanes to take it. Ahead and behind, the road was blessedly free of traffic. "The phone, now, please."

"I don't think so," she said, yelping when he reached across and grabbed it out of her hand.

She slumped defiantly into her seat, arms crossed over her chest. Checking again for oncoming vehicles, he pried open the phone and removed the battery, tossed the case over the top of the car toward the ditch, the power supply to the side of the road a quarter mile away.

"What the hell are you doing?" she screamed, whirling on him, fists flying, nails raking, grabbing for the steering wheel.

He hit the brakes, whipped into the skid. The fast stop and shoulder strap slammed her back into the bucket. He kept her there with the barrel of the Ruger .45-caliber he snatched from beneath his seat. "Sit down. Nothing's going to happen to you if you sit down and be still."

She didn't say a word, but he heard her hyperventilating panic above the roar in his ears.

"Calm down, Natasha. Listen to me. No one's going to get hurt." His pulse pounded. His mind whirred. "I just need you to be still and be quiet."

"You're pointing a gun at me and you want me to be still and be quiet? You fucking piece of shit." She swiped back the hair from her face. "Don't tell me to be still and be quiet. In fact, don't tell me anything at all. When Susan doesn't hear from me later, she's calling the cops. She knows exactly where we are and what we're driving. So whatever the hell you think you're doing here, you're not getting away with it. You lying, fucking bastard."

He caught her gaze, saw the glassy fear, the damp tears she wouldn't shed, the delineated vessels in the whites of her eyes like a road map penned in red. He wanted to tell her the truth, that he was one of the good guys, to reassure her that she could trust him, that no harm would come her way—but he couldn't tell her any of that and he refused to compound his sins with yet another lie.

And so he issued a growling order. "Shut the hell up, Natasha. Now."

Grabbing his phone from his belt, he punched in a preset code. The phone rang once. Julian Samms picked up the other end. "Shoot."

"I need to get to the farm. Where's Briggs?"

"Hang," Julian ordered, and Christian waited while his

SG-5 partner contacted Hank's chopper pilot, waited and watched Natasha hug herself with shaking hands, tears finally and silently rolling down her cheeks.

"I've got you on GPS. Briggs can be there in thirty, but you need to bank the car. And he needs a place to land. Hang."

More waiting. More looking for approaching cars. More watching Natasha glare, shake, and cry.

Christian switched from handset to earphone and lowered the gun to his thigh, keeping his gaze on Natasha while waiting for Julian's instructions. She seemed so small, so wounded, and he kicked himself all over again for failing to make it clear that their involvement was purely physical.

He should have spelled that out from day one, made it more clear that Peter Deacon took trophies, not lovers. But he'd never given her any such warning. Not that it would've done any good. Hell, he knew the lay of the land and here he was, so tied up in knots over what he was putting her through that he couldn't even think straight.

"My name is Christian Bane," he finally said, owing her that much. "That's all I can tell you right now."

She snorted, flipped him the bird, and turned to stare out her window.

"Bane."

"Yeah." Hand to his earpiece, he turned his attention back to Julian.

"Two miles ahead on the right," Julian said as Christian shifted into gear and accelerated, "there's a cutoff. Through a gate. Looks like a dirt road, rutted as hell."

He brought the car up to speed, scanned the landscape. "Got it," he said, and made the turn, nearly bottoming out on the first bump.

"Half a mile, make another right. Other side of a stand of trees."

"Almost there." He reached the cutoff and turned again,

caught sight of the tumbledown barn and stables, the flat pasture beyond. Perfect. Plenty of room for the chopper and cover for the car. "Tell Briggs we're waiting."

A short couple of seconds, and Julian said, "He says make it twenty. K.J.'s with him. He'll bring back the car. I'll keep the line open. Hank's expecting you."

"Thanks, J."

Christian maneuvered the Ferrari down the road that wasn't much more than a trail of flattened grass leading to a clearing surrounding the barn. Once he'd circled behind it, he tugged the wire from his ear, cut the engine, and pocketed the keys. When he opened his door, Natasha finally looked over.

"Going someplace?" she asked snidely.

"We both are," he bit back. "Get out."

"You can go to hell, but I'm not going anywhere."

"Actually, you are. And you're going with me." He reminded her that he was the one with the gun.

She got out of the car, slammed the door, and was off like a rocket back down the road. Shit, shit, shit. He checked the safety, shoved the Ruger into his waistband next to the SIG, and took off after her. She was fast, but he was faster. He closed in, but she never slowed, leaving him no choice.

He grabbed her arm. She spun toward him. He took her to the ground, bracing himself for the blow. He landed hard on his shoulder, doing what he could to cushion her fall. She grunted at the impact, and he rolled on top of her, pinning her to the ground with his weight and his strength.

Her adrenaline made for a formidable foe. She shoved at his chest, pummeled him with her fists when he refused to move. He finally had no choice but to grab her wrists, stretch out her arms above her head, hold her there.

Rocks and dirt and twigs bit into his fingers. He knew she felt the bite in the backs of her hands, but still he straddled her, capturing her legs between his.

"You want to wait like this? Twenty minutes? Because we can." His chest heaved in sync with the rapid rise and fall of hers. "Or we can get up and wait at the car. I'm good either way. You tell me."

"Get off me." She spat out the words.

He rolled up and away, kept his hands on her wrists and pulled her to her feet. Then he tugged her close, making sure he had her full attention, ignoring the stabbing pain in his shoulder that didn't hurt half as much as the one in his gut. "I'm not going to put up with any shit here, Natasha. Both of our lives are very likely in danger."

"Oh, right. I can see that. You being the one with the gun and all." She jerked her hands from his.

He let her go, walking a few feet behind her as she made her way slowly back to the barn and the parked car. She had nowhere to run; hopefully, he'd made his point. He had no intention to harm her, no *reason* to harm her, but he needed to finish this job, to make sure Spectra didn't get their hands on whatever it was Bow had to sell.

And now that he'd been stupid enough to get his cover blown . . .

"Where are you taking me?" She splayed shaking palms over the Ferrari's engine bay, staring down at her skin, which was ghostly pale against the car's black sheen.

"To get the answers you've been asking for," he said, guilt eating him from the inside out, and looked up with no small bit of relief at the *thwup-thwup-thwup* of an approaching chopper.

And also available from Brava—

THE SHAUGHNESSEY ACCORD

Tripp grabbed Glory by the shoulders, twirled her bodily across the room and into a tight corner where two of the shelving units met at a right angle.

"I know this part," she whispered as he wedged her inside. "Stay put."

He nodded, drew his gun and pressed his back to the wall at her side. The door slammed open and bounced off the cinderblocks behind. Tripp held the weapon raised, both hands at the ready, his heart doing a freight train run in his chest.

Beside him, Glory barely breathed. The shelf of supplies to his right blocked his view of the door but didn't keep his nostrils from flaring, his neck hairs from bristling, his adrenaline from pumping like gasoline.

He sensed their visitor long before the black-garbed man swung around and aimed his gun straight at Glory's head. The intruder stepped over his own downed associate and held out a gloved hand.

"Give me the gun and she will not die."

Tripp cursed violently under his breath, weighing his options on a different scale than he would've used in this situation had Glory not been involved.

If he'd had time to do more than react, time to think, plot and plan, he would've stashed the gun behind a can of olives and used the butt end to up his own prisoner count when the time was right.

Instead, he found himself surrendering the very piece that would've gone a long way to protecting Glory from this thug. But he was stuck using nothing but the wits that never seemed to operate at full throttle unless he had a contingency plan.

Right now all he had was a gut full of bile. That and a big fat regret that he didn't think better on his feet than he did.

Having passed over the gun, he raised both hands, palms out. "Let's neither of us go off half-cocked here."

The other man considered him for a long, strange moment, his black eyes broadcasting zero emotion while he stared for what seemed like forever before he tugged the ski mask from his head.

He was young. Tripp would've guessed twenty-three, twenty-four. Except when he looked at the kid's eyes. His expression was so dark, so blank, so unfeeling that it was like looking at a long-dead corpse.

Without moving his gaze from Tripp's, the kid shouted sharp orders in Vietnamese. Two other similarly garbed goons entered the storeroom and dragged away the dead weight Tripp had left in the middle of the floor.

Once the cast of extras was gone, the lead player planted his feet and shifted his gaze between Tripp and Glory, both hands hanging at his sides, one worrying the ski mask into a black fabric ball, the other flexed and ready and holding the gun.

"An interesting situation we find ourselves in here, isn't it?" he finally asked. "Miss Brighton, would you introduce me to your friend?"

"What do you want?" she asked before Tripp could stop

her. "Tell me what you want. I'll give it to you, and you can get out of my shop."

His black hair fell over his brow. "If what I have come for was so easily obtained, then I would have it in my possession by now."

He was after whatever the courier from the diamond exchange had delivered to the Spectra agent. Tripp was sure of it. Was sure as well the information would detail future packets removed from Sierra Leone.

The ski mask fell to the floor. "I'm waiting, Miss Brighton."

"He's a friend. A customer." Her hands fluttered at her waist. "We're just . . . good friends."

"You allow all your customers to visit your storeroom?" His mouth twisted cruelly. "Or only the ones with whom you are intimate?"

Glory gasped. Tripp placed his arm in front of her, a protective barrier he knew did little good. "C'mon, man. There's no need to go there."

The Asian kid raised a brow. "Actually, I think there is. Getting what I want often requires me to explore a defense's most vulnerable link. It is not always pleasant, but it can be quite effective." '

Tripp was pissed and rapidly getting more so. "Well, there are no links here to explore. So do as the lady suggested. Take what you've come for and let us all get back to our lives."

"Were it only so simple," he said as he gestured Glory forward. She forced her way past the barricade of Tripp's arm. "But we seem to have hit what will no doubt be an endlessly long impasse thanks to one of Miss Brighton's customers."

Glory looked from the kid back to Tripp, her eyes asking questions to which he had zero answers. "I don't understand."

"You are very predictable, Miss Brighton. As is your customer base. Same sandwiches. Same lunch hours. That made planning this job quite easy. I'm assuming the courier using your place of business for a drop point found your tight schedule advantageous, too."

Tripp's mind raced like the wind. The kid was talking way too much. His gang had blacked out the shop's single security camera, had made entry without alerting anyone to their presence, had secured the scene and done it all while Tripp made love to Glory.

Trip had been monitoring the shop for weeks and he'd never noticed the shop being scouted. He hadn't been wise to the intrusion until the kid had shot the lock off the door.

A guy who followed through on such flawless planning didn't start yapping his flap unless he felt there would be no survivors but him. And Tripp had a feeling they were looking into the dead eyes of an animal who'd fight to the death before being taken alive.

Here's a preview of

THE BEACH ALIBI

He couldn't believe it.

He *abso-fucking-lutely* couldn't believe this was happening. Not here. Not now.

He'd prepped for this mission for weeks. He knew every way into this building, every way out. Windows, elevators, ducts, doors, all of it.

How the hell could he have missed the goddamn camera hidden in the wall clock?

Kelly John Beach averted his head, stared at his shoes, at the pine green-and-navy leaf pattern in the executive suite's carpet beneath, ordered himself to think, think, *think*.

The camera was new. He hadn't missed it. The clock hadn't been here before tonight. He'd scanned this office an hour after the cleaning crew had left, doing an electronic sweep while in uniform as building security.

There had been nothing, *nothing*, on that wall other than the CFO's flat panel television.

That didn't change the fact that now there was. Or the fact that the position he was in was more than compromising.

It was neck-in-the noose illegal.

The CD of classified Spectra IT intel he'd come for was tucked safely into the vest strapped to his chest. Getting out of here wasn't going to be a problem. He'd simply reverse the trip he'd made coming in.

The trouble would come later.

Three minutes from now, he'd be ground level wearing street clothes. Give the cops another thirty, he'd be wearing handcuffs.

God-fucking-damn.

Sweat beaded on his forehead, rolled like Niagara down his spine. His eyeballs burned. His temples throbbed. His heart was a fist-size red rubber ball clogging the base of his throat.

He had to get to the SG-5 ops center without hitting the street. The only way to do that was the subway at the Broad Street station. Then underground.

He hated going underground. He hated the dark. Hated the rats. Hated the stench of shit and decay and all the rotten crap he'd have to step in.

Right, he growled, grumbled, snorted. Now he was really looking forward to the trip. But a man had to do what a man had to do, or so went the saying.

And so he did. Sucked it up, swallowed his own bullshit and the red rubber ball, and walked out of the Spectra IT office like the fucking President of the U.S. of A.

"Slow it down, son. Slow it down." Hank Smithson gestured toward Kelly John with the stub end of a cigar tucked in the crook of his index finger. "You're not going to get this figured out by wearing a hole in the floor."

The older man could use his calming techniques all he wanted. Kelly John wasn't in any mood to be calmed or gentled or put out to pasture. Not when it looked like he was about to be put down.

He paced the SG-5 ops center's huge horseshoe workstation from his own desk to Tripp Shaughnessey's and back. Again and again and again.

"Easy for you to say." He stopped, sniffed. Christ, but he smelled like a freakin' sewer. "You aren't the one who screwed up."

It was more than screwing up the mission and giving Spectra the upper hand. It was letting down the others, exposing the Smithson Group.

Failing Hank.

Hank crossed his arms over his chest and rocked back on his boot heels. "Kelly, you did your best."

His best hadn't been good enough. Not this time. A hell of a hard pill to swallow considering the reason Hank had picked him to join the Smithson Group in the first place. "They had to know I was coming. That's the only way the timing of that camera install makes sense."

"They were protecting their assets," Hank reminded him.

A reminder that pissed him off even further when he thought of the source of the organization's millions. "Yeah, well, now they've got video proving how insecure they really are. And how stupid I really am."

Hank moved, blocking Kelly John's path, commanding his attention. "We'll figure it out, son. We'll figure it out."

"What's to figure?"

At Tripp Shaughnessey's offhanded question, both men turned, Kelly John glaring down at his partner where Tripp sat on the floor in front of his desk. "What the hell's that supposed to mean?"

Tightening the wheels on his upended chair, Tripp shrugged. "You're the computer whiz. Make your own video. Prove you were elsewhere at the time. Show them they only think they know what they're seeing."

"An alibi," Hank said.

Intrigued, Kelly John started pacing again. "That might work."

"And we all know who would make the best alibi, right?" Tripp asked.

Something in Tripp's tone told Kelly John he wasn't going to like the answer. "Who?"

"A woman."

And here's a peek at

THE McKENZIE ARTIFACT

The drapes over his motel room's window pulled open, Eli McKenzie stood and stared through the mottled glass, squinting at the starburst shards of sunlight reflected off the windshields of the cars barreling down Highway 90 in the distance.

Second floor up meant he could see Del Rio, Texas, on the horizon, and to his left a silvery sliver of the twisting Rio Grande, a snake reminding him of the venom he'd be facing once he harnessed the guts to cross.

The room's cooling unit blew tepid air up his bare torso, making a weak attempt at drying the persistent sheet of sweat. Sweat having less to do with the heat of the day than with the choking memory of the poison he'd unknowingly ingested on his last trip here.

An accidental ingestion. A purposeful poisoning.

Someone in Mexico wanted him dead.

The only surprise there was that no one but Rabbit knew Eli's true identity. Wanting to dispose of an SG-5 operative was one thing, but he hadn't been made. Which meant this was personal.

This was about his covert identity, his posing as a member of the Spectra IT security team guarding the compound across the border.

An identity he'd lived and breathed for six months until the nausea and dysarthria, the diarrhea, ataxia and tremors turned him into a monster. One everyone around him wanted to kill.

He'd tried himself. Once.

Rabbit had stopped him and sent him back to New York and to Hank Smithson, the Smithson Group principal, to heal. Eli owed both men his life, though it was his debt to Hank that weighed heaviest.

Hank, who plucked men in need of redemption off their personal highways to hell and set them down on roads less traveled. Roads that took the SG-5 operatives places not a one of them wished to see again after reaching the end of their missions.

Places like the Spectra IT compound in Mexico.

Scratching the center of his chest, Eli shook his head and pondered his immediate future. He and Rabbit were the only ones inside the compound not working for Spectra. Outside was a different story.

And there had been one person nosing around and causing enough scenes to make a movie.

Stella Banks.

Stella Banks with her platinum blonde hair and battered straw cowboy hat and legs longer than split rail fence posts. She was an enigma. A private investigator who dressed like a barrel racer and looked like a runway model.

She kept an office in Ciudad Acuna, another in Del Rio. He knew she was working the disappearance of her office manager's daughter, Carmen Garcia. The girl was four-teen, and like so many of the others gone missing recently, a beauty.

She was also currently being held inside the compound,

waiting to be shipped away from her family and into a life of prostitution courtesy of Spectra IT. Or so had been the case last Eli had checked in with Rabbit.

The room wasn't getting any cooler, the day any longer, the truth of what lay ahead any easier to swallow. Like it or not, it was time to go. Once across the border, he'd make his way south a hundred kilometers in the heap Rabbit had left parked in a field west of the city.

As much as Eli longed for a haircut and a shave, he wouldn't bother with either. The scruffy disguise went a long way to helping him blend in, to hiding the disgust he never quite wiped from his face.

Considering the condition of the car and the roads, he was looking at a good two hours of travel time. One hundred and twenty minutes to go over the plans he'd worked out with Rabbit to take down these bastards.

Plans trickier than Eli liked to deal with but which couldn't be helped. Not with the lives of twenty teenaged girls on the line.

He hadn't quite nailed down his plans for Stella Banks.

He needed her out of the way.

Before he got rid of her, however, he needed to find out what she and her outside sources could add to what Rabbit had learned on the inside.

Only then would Eli make certain she never interfered in his mission again.

He was alive.

And he was back.

That son-of-a-bitch was back.

Stella Banks curled her fingers through the chain links of the fenced enclosure and watched him leave the compound's security office and cross the yard to the barracks.

She couldn't believe it. Not after all the trouble she'd gone through—and gotten into—to get rid of his sorry kidnapping ass for good.

Next time she'd forgo the poison and use a bullet instead.